EBURY PR

NALA DAMAYANTI

Anand Neelakantan is the author of the Bahubali trilogy, the official prequel to S.S. Rajamouli's movie. The first book in the series, *The Rise of Sivagami*, was released in 2017, and was a bestseller across all charts for two years and was on Amazon's list of top five bestsellers for 2017. The second book, *Chaturanga*, and the final book in the trilogy, *Queen of Mahishmati*, were subsequently published with outstanding success. Netflix has announced a series based on the Bahubali trilogy.

Anand debuted as an author in 2012 with his iconic book *Asura: Tale of the Vanquished*, which told the tale of Ramayana from the perspective of Ravana. The book has been translated into sixteen languages and is on Amazon's '100 Books to Be Read in a Lifetime' list. Anand followed it up with the hugely popular Ajaya series, a retelling of the Mahabharata from Duryodhana's point of view. *Vanara*, published by Penguin, told the story of the Ramayana from Baali's perspective and became an instant bestseller. The book is slated to be a major motion picture and was optioned for one of the biggest bids in the Indian film industry.

Anand also wrote the popular children's book *The Very, Extremely, Most Naughty Asura Tales for Kids*, published by Puffin. There is an upcoming animation series based on this book. He has also published a short-story collection titled *Valmiki's Women*. Anand's audiobook, *Many Ramayanas, Many Lessons*, was in the top three listens of Audible India in 2021 and 2022. *Nala Damayanti* first appeared as an audio drama in Storytel in ten languages and became Storytel's most-listened-to book in 2022.

Anand is a prolific screenplay writer and has written hugely popular series like *Siya Ke Ram*, *Chakravarthi Samrat Ashoka*, *Mahabali Hanuman*, *Sarfrosh*, *Adaalat*, *Taj* and *Swaraj*, among others. Ace director Rakeysh Omprakash Mehra has announced a two-part film based on the Mahabharata that Anand is co-writing with him. Reliance Entertainment has announced a spy thriller for a major OTT channel with Anand as the lead writer.

For the past six years, Anand has been writing a regular fortnightly column, named Acute Angle, for the *New Indian Express*. Anand also writes in Malayalam and has authored a short-story collection, travelogues, articles and film reviews for leading Malayalam dailies. Anand dabbles in cartooning, painting, public speaking, life coaching, acting and modelling. He lives in Mumbai with his family.

Celebrating 35 Years of
Penguin Random House India

NALA
DAMAYANTI

An Eternal Tale from the Mahabharata

ANAND
NEELAKANTAN

EBURY
PRESS

An imprint of Penguin Random House

EBURY PRESS

USA | Canada | UK | Ireland | Australia
New Zealand | India | South Africa | China

Ebury Press is part of the Penguin Random House group of companies
whose addresses can be found at global.penguinrandomhouse.com

Published by Penguin Random House India Pvt. Ltd
4th Floor, Capital Tower 1, MG Road,
Gurugram 122 002, Haryana, India

Penguin
Random House
India

First published as an audiobook by Storytel Original IN 2022
Published in Ebury Press by Penguin Random House India 2023

ISBN 9780143453536

Typeset in Bembo Std by Manipal Technologies Limited, Manipal

www.penguin.co.in

Contents

1

The Golden Bird

Brahma woke up from aeons of cosmic sleep and discovered that he had made a mistake. He was horrified. Just when he was about to correct the error with a snap of his fingers, Hemanga held his hand.

'Oh leave me, bird,' Brahma cried. 'Let me do what is appropriate. The last of my creations are abominable. It affronts me as an artist that I ever even conceived it.'

'Father, you designed the Universe, vast and infinite. In a little corner, you placed a pale blue dot. You filled the earth with air and added a drop of love to it. It changed everything. Life sprouted. From the twinkle of your eyes, spring came. You made the cuckoo sing the song of love, the peacock dance to summon the rain, and the breeze to carry the heady fragrance of mango blossoms. You created parijatha, sapthaparnis, chembaka, kadamba, and so many other fragrant flowers. You made birds and beasts, grass, and trees . . . '

Brahma said, shaking his three heads, the past, the present and the future, 'Alas, my last stroke spoilt the art.'

'Humans are magnificent,' Hemanga said, referring to Brahma's finishing touch in his creation.

'Don't insult me,' Brahma cried, 'ignoble creatures . . . I am sick of them. Hemanga, look what these obnoxious creatures are doing.' And with that, Brahma waved his hand and before Hemanga's eyes, appeared a vision of what humans called the civilization.

'Watch those fools,' Brahma cried, pointing to a group of people dancing in front of a temple. Hemanga bent forward to look closely. The dancing people had pierced their skins with needles. Some had a mini trident impaled through their cheeks. Others were rolling on the ground, chanting mantras and praising God. 'And now look at these,' Brahma swore and apologized for his Sanskrit. A mendicant was standing upside down, chanting something. Another stood on one leg near him, mumbling gibberish and, as the scene expanded, Hemanga could see thousands of such people in acrobatic positions.

'What are they doing?' Hemanga asked.

'They are trying to please me,' Brahma said, 'and look at those morons!'

With a flick of his wrist, the scene changed. It was another part of the earth. A mob was chasing a woman, hurling stones at her and baying for her blood. 'That woman spoke against me. Their sentiments are hurt, and they are out lynching people. All in my name.'

'Well, some of them are certainly mad,' Hemanga said slowly, defensively.

Brahma said, 'None of them have tried to know me, yet they fight in my name. These creatures have become a nuisance, a nag. They don't let me sleep. They are at it without pause, beseeching me, "Oh God, give me this, give me that!" Argh. I am fed up! I cannot not even sleep well because of their nagging.'

'You were sleeping for many aeons,' Hemanga said. Brahma glowered at the bird, 'I didn't ask your opinion,' he retorted. He was about to snap his fingers and annihilate humans, when Hemanga cried, 'Please . . .!'

'Hemanga, you would never understand my pain. Their incessant beseeching haunt even my dreams. This, after doing the most obnoxious thing—they have devised their own God: Kali.'

'Are you jealous that they pray to him instead of you?'

'Bah! Who wants their prayer or praise? But they have this God created from their own fears. They believe Kali controls their fate. And they think it is my duty to save them from Kali. Argh, what a bunch of morons I have created! Greed, selfishness, anger, envy, pride, laziness—these define my last creation. I must have been in a bad mood when I created humans. Or insane. I should wipe all humans forever and remove the blot from my masterpiece.'

Hemanga cried, 'No, no, no, no. Please . . . father! No. Somewhere out there, is pure love. In some place, somewhere that you don't know, there must be selfless human beings. I believe, I truly believe, that there has to be that someone who will laugh at the face of Kali. Allow me to find them for you. It is not for the artist to decide the worth of his creation, but for the connoisseurs of art. What if humans are your real masterpiece?'

'Then I have no prospect of ever being a true artist,' Brahma said, a slight shudder escaping him.

'Even mistakes are beautiful in art, my father. Let me find the best among them for you. I have asked nothing from you before. Please give them a chance . . . for my sake,' Hemanga pleaded.

The creator sat running his fingers through his long white beard for a while. Hemanga wondered whether Brahma was having one of his famous long sleep. At last, Brahma opened his six eyes and said, 'Show me that there is at least one man and woman whose love doesn't whither with the loss of fortune, fame, good looks, or power. Show me someone who Kali cannot defeat, and I shall rethink my decision.'

Hemanga kissed the creator fervently and flew out.

When Hemanga informed his family about his decision to leave for earth, his parents were aghast. No one trusted humans. *'They will kill you,'* his mother cried. His father was angry, 'You will return disillusioned,' he forewarned, adding, 'Instead of wasting your time on such impossible missions, why couldn't you concentrate on becoming the head Swan of Manasarovara?'

Hemanga had no answer.

Later he overheard his father moaning to other sympathetic friends, 'My son is going for a wild-goose chase at a time when I was looking forward to my retirement.'

And of course, those uncles and aunties, who Brahma had created mainly for poking their noses in the affairs of other people's children and giving them unsolicited advice, tried to dissuade Hemanga. 'Son, if you insist on going abroad, there is Swarga of Devas and there is Patala of Asuras,' they said. 'Why do you want to go to Earth? It is a third world.'

Apparently, saving the human race was not a career with any future for a young swan. However, it was time to leave. Polite but firm, the bird flew to earth, leaving an angry father and distressed mother behind. And, even though the uncle and aunt swans of Manasarovara shook their heads in dismay, they were secretly happy their children were not like Hemanga.

* * *

The golden swan travelled across *lokas,* from the snow-filled mountains to the distant pearl islands that floated on turquoise green seas. He saw oceans of shining sands where nothing grew except for date palms and thorny cacti, to steamy jungles and rocky wastelands. Earth was heart-achingly beautiful.

Then he encountered humans. 'Was Brahma right?' he wondered in dismay. He saw men and women who were tall or short, pale yellow, brown or dark of skin, who worshipped different Gods and believed in the varied stories that poets among them had made up as true. Yet they all were the same. In none did the golden swan find anyone worthy of altruistic love.

The shadow of Kali loomed large over them all. The God they had created from their fears was now controlling their minds and directing their actions.

Just when Hemanga was losing hope, he met a sage.

'There are only a few humans who can take on Kali,' the sage told him.

'I couldn't find even one,' scoffed Hemanga.

'Well, have you heard about Nala?' asked the sage.

'Nala? Who is he?'

That is all the sage needed to start talking about the virtues of Nala. When the sage finished, Hemanga said thoughtfully, 'That is wonderful, but it is hard to believe he has no flaws.'

'Well, he is the King of Nishadas.'

The Nishadas were forest dwellers. Hemanga was piqued, instantly. 'How could that be a flaw?' he cried.

'He is a low caste,' the sage's eyes twinkled with mischief. Hemanga pondered over it and asked, 'What is caste?'

'It is too complicated to explain.'

'Try me.'

'I shall put it like this: Among humans, it is the circumstance of birth and not the quality of deeds that determine who is noble and who is not. Some call it caste, some reason it as race, but the essence is the same. Your birth determines your superiority.'

'That is so stupid!' *How could humans be superior or inferior to each other,* he wanted to ask. *How could one set of people be shunned by another set for no reason other than some rules that humans themselves made? Was Brahma right?*

'The humans have created Kali, the God of fate, and are now scared of him. Maybe you should go back and encourage Brahma to click his fingers in a trice. It is not worth saving these fools.'

'So, are you saying that no woman would love Nala, despite his qualities?'

'Well, to challenge Kali, perhaps only the Princess of Vidarbha is there. She is intelligent and beautiful. Her name is Damayanti and there is no man worthy of her, not even Nala.'

'Ah, then I could bring them together and a new race would emerge that would be wise and . . .'

'As if Kali would let you do that,' the sage smiled.

'I will try. Else, humans have no hope.'

'Good luck,' the sage said. 'And here is one tip. The best way to unite Nala and Damayanti is through food.'

'Food?' Hemanga asked, perplexed.

'Nala is the greatest cook to have ever lived,' Narada said and blessed Hemanga.

Then Narada Muni, a mischief maker, watched the bird fly to the land of Nishadas and chuckled. Had Hemanga realized who the sage was, he would not have ventured into such a hopeless mission. Little did the bird know that he had consulted the sage of troubles.

The game was on and prankster Narada had to get the other stakeholder to participate in the challenge. Dusting his hands, chanting, 'Narayana, Narayana,' with a satisfied chuckle, Narada set out to serendipitously meet Kali and warn him about the bird from paradise.

Now the fun would begin.

2

Damayanti

When Hemanga saw Damayanti for the first time, he wished that the creator had made him a human instead of a swan. The poets were not exaggerating. He had seen no woman, neither in the heavenly abode of devas nor in the netherworld of asuras, who was as stunning as Damayanti.

Hiding in the canopy of the chembaka tree in her garden, Hemanga watched the princess. In the delightful breeze of the spring, her long tresses swayed like blades of grass in a meadow. Her dark eyes sparkled with mischief and a zest for life. Hemanga watched as she strolled in the garden with her friends. There was something arresting about her voice—like a bubbling brook. Just listening to her laugh brought a surge of happiness. She went past Hemanga's hiding place and the swan followed her, panting and puffing, cursing the cold breeze that made him shiver. Who in the right mind would prefer to walk in this weather when all one would want was to snuggle in a bed of feathers?

Hemanga sighed, hopelessly in love. Damayanti was standing at the steps of the lotus pond and she looked like a sculpture that had come alive. Her long, thick hair, her large, long lashed eyes, her sharp nose, her slim waist, her clear skin, her dimpled smile . . . Hemanga couldn't take his eyes off her. She paused to smile at the little worms that dangled from leaves, to coo to the cuckoo and to feed the fish. The swan darted from bush to bush, gazing at the princess as she stood watching the dewdrop that hung on the tip of flower petals. He followed her as Damayanti treaded softly over the grass, tracing the path of a dragonfly. And as she sat lazily on a rock, her feet dangling in water, her eyes dreamy in contemplation, Hemanga continued watching from a distance. The swan could hear the murmur of poetry in the breeze. It was bliss to behold someone who radiated so much joy just as it was terrifying.

Did she really need a man?

A scream startled the celestial bird from its romantic reverie. The princess was wading deeper through the freezing water of the lake and the female palace staff were pleading with her to return. She ducked underwater and disappeared, leaving ripples of water to spiral out. The bird took off, scanning the water surface, looking out for Damayanti. He saw her swimming some distance away. A small island loomed ahead; half hidden in the mist. An egret burst out from the tangles of water lilies and shrieked past his ears, leaving Hemanga startled. He hurled abuses at the egret, which circled and landed in the water, a few feet away.

When Hemanga turned, the princess was already in the island and walking towards the bush. Hemanga hurried towards her and when he saw what she was up to, he screamed in terror, 'Don't!'

Damayanti smiled at him and extended her hand to the bush. The cobra struck like lightning, but the princess was quicker. She retracted her extending hand. The cobra spread its hood and regarded her with its cold eyes. Hemanga caught hold of Damayanti's ankle and tried to pull her back.

'Don't be afraid. The poor creature has got stuck in the thorn bush. Let me help it,' she said, gently pushing him away.

As she extended her hand and the snake lashed out, Hemanga found himself cringing, his eyes shut. When he opened his eyes, the cobra was safely coiled in Damayanti's wrist. She walked to the water and Hemanga followed, babbling incoherently. Damayanti set the snake free and stood watching the silver line the snake left in its wake as it swam towards its freedom.

'You almost got killed,' Hemanga glowered at her. Damayanti stared at him.

'You . . . you can talk?' Damayanti shrieked in surprise.

'Well, I have been crying hoarse, warning you never to meddle with those obnoxious creatures. Cobras are nasty. And that cobra you rescued was no ordinary cobra. There was something sinister about it. It meant real harm.'

Damayanti squeaked, 'You can really speak.'

The swan rolled his huge eyes, 'Of course, I can speak. I was pleading with you not to touch those . . . '

'But you can talk like a human, how wonderful!'

'I have been talking for quite some time and you were . . . ' Hemanga's voice trailed as realization dawned on him. His head dropped in shame.

'Why are you silent, have you swallowed something?' Damayanti chuckled.

'I am swallowed by shame, Devi,' Hemanga stammered, struggling with embarrassment. 'My apologies. When one is excited . . . agitated . . . or . . . uhm . . . a little bit . . . well . . . er . . . afraid . . . one falls back into speaking one's mother tongue. I might have talked in swan tongue to you in my . . . er . . . excitement.'

Damayanti laughed and gently touched his golden head, 'Are you for real? A talking swan?'

Hemanga stammered, 'I . . . I . . . er . . . am from Manasarovara, the lake of Brahma.'

'What? You are again talking in swan tongue, are you . . . excited?' Damayanti threw her head and laughed in delight.

Hemanga blushed deeper, 'Er . . . No. No. No, not at all Devi.' He realized that he was still talking in swan tongue and switched to say, 'I am a messenger.'

'A messenger?'

Hemanga bowed gracefully and said, 'A messenger of love, Devi.'

Damayanti chuckled, 'What does that even mean?'

'I will find the perfect one for you,' Hemanga said.

'And let me guess. You are the perfect one!'

Hemanga was blushing so much that he did not want to turn towards her. When she came around to face him, he turned on his heel hiding his face with his extended wings.

Eying her through the gap in his feathers, Hemanga said, 'I am a humble swan. I come with the message of love from the perfect man.' He saw Damayanti blush. Beads of perspiration lined her brows. Hemanga felt a pang of jealousy in his heart. If only Brahma had made him a human. Sighing, he pushed away that thought.

Damayanti laughed aloud, 'This is the funniest thing I have heard in my life. Do you know my father has fixed my *swayamvara*? My father Bhimasena, the King of Vidarbha, has invited all the princes from the entire Bharathavarsha for it.'

Hemanga blinked. 'What is a swayamvara?' he asked.

'I will choose one of the men among these noble princes as my husband on a particular day.'

'Then you should choose Nala,' Hemanga said.

'It is a swayamvara. My choice. And I don't even know who he is. Why should I marry him just because a strange bird is telling me to do so?'

This was the chance Hemanga was waiting for so long. He had been ready to talk—nay, sing paeans—about the man he saw as the perfect one. He cleared his throat.

'What are you doing?' She asked perplexed.

'I am going to sing about that man, that wonderful man, that perfect man,' the swan hopped on to a rock and spread his wings to the winter sun. 'Nala—the handsome, the brave, the generous . . . ' he crooned.

Damayanti closed her ears with her palms, 'Enough!'

'I have not even begun!'

'Has anyone told you have a harsh voice?' Damayanti asked and Hemanga's face fell. 'No one has told me,' he responded petulantly. 'Everyone loves my singing. But it seems you don't like my song.'

'Well, swans are not famous for their sweet voices. You can *tell* me about your hero. Just. Don't. Sing.'

'Who says swans can't sing? Do you know there is a raga named after us? Hamsadhwani, the melodious voice of swans. So, sing I shall, croon I shall, the paeans of Nala, the Nishada,' Hemanga argued hotly.

'Wait! What? A Nishada?' Damayanti exclaimed.

'Yes, the King of Nishadas.'

'You think I will marry a Nishada?' Damayanti asked.

'Why not?'

Damayanti rolled her eyes and said, 'And what are the other qualities of this king of hunter tribes?'

The sarcasm was wasted on the golden bird. 'He is the greatest cook who has ever lived.'

Damayanti snickered, 'What! What . . . a cook?'

'Yes, they say he can make anything taste good. Give him a stone and he will add a dollop of cow butter, stir it in slow fire, sprinkle in pepper and ginger, stew it in milk, garnish it with cinnamon and serve with fresh yam fry. And ta-dah! The stone will melt in your mouth. That is the culinary skill of Nala.'

'I don't want to eat stones, however well cooked.'

'The stone was just a figure of speech. A poetic exaggeration. But he is a wonderful cook,' Hemanga said.

'Why should I care for a king who is not a warrior?' scoffed the princess. 'Has he conquered other kingdoms? Has he conducted Aswamedha, the horse sacrifice?'

'There are so many kings in the world who can fight battles and kill thousands of men. They can crumble the cities, annihilate civilizations and trample many under the hooves of their cavalry. They can torch granaries, burn the old and the invalid, create widows and orphans . . . If that is your scale of measuring a man's greatness, then Nala is not great. He is a simple man, who is generous, kind, and compassionate.'

'I have not even met the man. Am I supposed to believe the words of a strange swan that talks in human tongue? What if you are the pet bird of Nala? So, thank you, talking bird, but I would prefer to choose my husband myself.'

'But he loves you,' Hemanga said plaintively.

'Oh, is it?' Damayanti asked, 'and what is the proof? You said you are a messenger. Where is the message?'

Hemanga panicked. He had yet to meet Nala. He had no clue whether Nala would fall in love with this woman. He had blindly trusted Narada, the troublemaker, and now he was in a fix.

'I . . . I will bring his message,' Hemanga stammered.

'Oh, so you have no message to give now,' Damayanti laughed. 'Tell me the truth, bird. Does such a man even exist?'

'I will bring a token of love from him,' Hemanga said.

Half in jest and half in an attempt to get rid of the swan, Damayanti agreed to receive a gift from Nala and shooed the bird away.

Hemanga had no clue how he was going to convince Nala about Damayanti. He never knew being the messenger of love was such a risky profession. 'I should have listened to my father's advice,' thought the golden swan as he flew to the Nishada land.

3

The Nishada Country

Hemanga had no clue how he would convince Nala about marrying Damayanti. All through his flight, he kept rifling through his head for a plan. And there was something that kept nagging him. His mind kept thinking of the cobra that Damayanti had rescued from the thorn bush. *That was no ordinary snake.* He was sure of it. Pushing away the dark thoughts that were gathering in his mind, the golden swan flew to the Nishada country.

When he reached the country of Nala, the western sky had a tinge of blush. The bird circled the land of forest dwellers and the more he saw it, the more ecstatic he grew. Hundreds of temple domes sparkled in the rays of the setting sun. As he dove down towards the city, he could see a crowd had gathered before a temple. Even from the height he was flying, he could smell the aroma of some exotic food. Aha, a fire in the courtyard and a huge copper vessel resting on it. What was brewing?

The swan perched on a tree to watch. What was it that was making all the humans so excited? The vessel was humongous, almost as big as the lily pond near it. Milk was bubbling up from it while three men continued to stir it with huge ladles. A group of children sat around the fire, their eyes twinkling with anticipation. They had bowls in their hands and they banged them on the floor, creating a ruckus, 'Payasam, payasam, give us payasam.'

'Only after offering it to Brahma, greedy brats,' said an important-looking man.

'We want now, Prince Pushkara,' a boy cried. 'That is a recipe of our King Nala! We can't wait to have it! Please hurry up,' one of the children cried and others repeated his request.

'Do you want the curse of God Kali upon you?' Pushkara sneered and the children went silent. A priest chanted, 'God of Gods, Brahma Deva, take our offerings and save us from Kali.'

'There is no Kali, and Brahma wants none of your offerings,' Hemanga said, flying down gently and then sauntering towards the centre where the concoction was brewing.

'A golden bird,' the crowd gasped. Hemanga, who was always proud of his beautiful feathers, decided to put up a show. He spread his wings to the sun and said in a commanding tone, 'Call your King Nala and ask him to give me a token of love to carry to Damayanti. He should meet Damayanti quickly. There is going to be a swayamvara soon and it seems they won't invite Nishadas. He has no time to waste.' The crowd simply stared. No one moved. 'Why are you all staring at me?' demanded Hemanga, looking at everyone around him. 'Aren't you getting what I am saying?' Hemanga wondered whether he had squawked in swan tongue, instead of human.

'A talking swan,' someone gasped.

Hemanga bowed in relief. He was becoming an expert in human speech.

Then Pushkara said, 'He's worth a fortune.'

At once the implication of Pushkara's words dawned on him. 'Oh no!' Hemanga cried. 'No, no, no, no, no!' He backtracked as the prince took a step forward, beckoning the bird to come near him. 'I am not a chicken,' he scolded the prince with indignation. 'Don't go ba ba ba ba on me!' Walking backwards, his eyes firmly fixed on Pushkara, imitating his call, he heard something rustled behind him.

Hemanga took off just in time to find that he had barely escape the hands of a soldier who had sneaked up to him from behind. He perched on the highest tower of a temple and looked down at the people. They looked agitated. Some rushed out of their homes with bows and arrows. Things were getting serious.

'He would be delicious to eat,' a man yelled. Hemanga could hear scores of bows drawn and arrows notched. An arrow whisked past him. The bird trembled in fear as one of the aimed arrows came close enough to dislodge a feather from his head. Many others had missed by a whisker.

'Whoa! I came up to save you and you want to make a barbecue of me? Such beautiful people you are!' Hemanga cried. The more he spoke, the more the commotion on the ground below increased.

Soon half a dozen young men were scampering up the temple tower. It was no longer safe to stay there. 'I am floored at your intelligence, wise people,' Hemanga cackled, 'Do you think I would be sitting here waiting for you monkeys to catch me? Do I look like a kitten? I have wings, folks. I am a bird.'

While he was talking, Hemanga did not notice that Prince Pushkara had sneaked up from the other side. Before he knew it, something had grabbed him by his feet.

'Got you!' Prince Pushkara grinned, jubilantly.

Hemanga said, 'King Nala should be ashamed to call you his brother. Do you know why? Because you are a fool.' Hemanga pecked hard on Pushkara's nose and the prince yelled in pain. He almost lost balance and grabbed the leg of a carved statue for his dear life. The free swan took off in a trice.

Hemanga hovered before Pushkara's eyes, 'A piece of advice, friend. Always catch a bird by its neck or you will get your nose pecked.'

Then yelling, 'Barbarians! Nincompoops!' he flew around an exquisitely carved temple towers while the angry Nishadas yelled at him and hurled stones and arrows.

Hemanga had enough of the Nishadas. Wondering whether Narada had played a prank on him by recommending Nala, Hemanga flew to hide in the jungles till he figured out a way to approach Nala. Had he looked behind, he would have seen a cobra slithering right after him.

4

Nala

Hemanga decided to learn everything about Nala and his people. The Nishadas were a tribe in the Vindhya mountains and hunting was how they had survived from the dawn of time. Nala had changed everything. He built their first city and brought agriculture to his tribe. He constructed granaries. He brought great sculptors from all parts of the world to build magnificent temples. Many musicians, artisans, dancers, and artists flocked to the Nishada kingdom over time.

The prosperity of Nala's country had created a wave of resentment and jealousy. Brahma had created Nishadas to hunt in the jungles and not to dwell in magnificent cities that valued scholars, artists, and musicians. How dare the low-born forest dwellers dream so big; worse, how could they achieve what the others could not even fathom? When the kings paid poets to sing their praises and to cook up stories about their lineage that stretched to the sun and the moon, King Nala of the Nishadas never hid his noble origins. He worked quietly to make his kingdom the most prosperous. He had no time for war, except to defend his kingdom and protect his people.

He had his detractors in his tribe too. There were old timers who missed the old way of life. They ruminated on the thrill of the hunt. They missed the freedom of the forest. 'We are now slaves of plants and cattle,' they sighed. 'From dawn to dusk, our king is making us tend them for a little milk or some grains,' they hissed in hushed tones. The vagaries of agriculture and the boredom of a settled life were not for them. They did not express their resentment openly, for Nala was popular and loved by most; but they bid their time.

The more Hemanga knew about Nala, the more he respected the gentle Nishada. But how would he convince Damayanti about his worth? She was a high-born princess, scion of a royal family. Why should she even look at a lowly Nishada? Hemanga had learnt that among humans, their inherent qualities did not matter. The accident of birth decided one's worth. Hemanga could not figure out a way to overcome this unique trait of humans. Among any other creations of Brahma, the might or capability would have decided the matter.

The other thing bothering Hemanga was that he couldn't help noticing that the snake was following him. The cobra neither hunted nor it slept. It was a constant presence, a shadow behind Hemanga. It kept watching him with its cruel eyes. *Could it read his mind?* Hemanga was convinced it could. The swan tried his best to ignore the cobra and find a way to unite Nala and Damayanti.

One day, when the snake was not visible and he was able to think with a calmer mind, Narada's words came back to him. *Nala was a great cook.* An idea started forming in his mind. It involved stealing and he was not comfortable with the plan. But time was running out and he had to do something.

* * *

Hemanga flew to the Nishada kingdom and sneaked to the roof. He could smell the aroma of something delicious wafting through the air. The royal kitchen was not difficult to find. He moved a roof tile and peered down. There was Nala, stirring a huge vat with a ladle. A couple of royal cooks stood in the corner with resentful faces. Their master had appropriated their profession, making them mere spectators.

Nala stirred the oil humming a song. The aroma from the stove made the swan giddy. Nala took out a ladle of spiral sweets dripping with butter and flicked them into a reed basket to drain off the oil. His handsome face shone. Hemanga took a deep breath, preparing to dive in and carry back some of these delectable creations from the very prince's hands. Damayanti, Hemanga was sure, would immediately fall in love with this handsome man if only she could taste what he cooked. It looked so appealing.

Hemanga carefully wriggled through the hole in the roof and flew inside. He snatched a sweet from the basket and in an instant, his brain felt struck by white pain. Dropping the scalding treat, the swan screeched in pain. He had burnt his beak. Blinded with agony, the bird spat out the savoury and dashed straight ahead . . . into the stove. The vat overturned, splashing boiling oil on Nala's toe. The king screamed. The servants screamed louder. Hemanga croaked and skidded blindly here and there. The cooks and servants dashed to catch the swan. The bird crashed into shelves, knocking down pots filled with spices.

And just like that the air was thick with the pungent smell of pepper. Frantic sneezing ensued from many noses. Men slipped on oil spills and fell with their faces buried in barrels of dough. Pots and pans toppled down. Over and above all the screaming and sneezing and howls of pain, was the scared screech of Hemanga as men chased the bird around the kitchen. Choking, eyes streaming with tears and sneezing, the bird desperately sought a way to escape.

When the commotion finally settled, men found themselves standing on a kitchen floor that was spewed with the wreck of broken pans and pots. Hemanga looked at the ridiculous figures of Nishadas covered in various powdered spices and dough, fuming at him. Some had turmeric in their hair with specks of chilly red. Some had a sooty face with dough-white hair.

Hemanga let out a nervous laugh and was about to offer a profuse apology when a grip tightened around his narrow neck, choking him.

'Well, who do we have here? The talking golden swan.' Pushkara raised Hemanga from the floor and shoved it at his brother's face. 'Brother, you said talking swans are stuffs of fairy tales when I told you about this one. Here he is.'

Hemanga tried to wriggle free and Pushkara's grip tightened. 'Speak,' he shook the bird.

'Leave it, Pushkara. The poor thing is hungry.'

'I am hungry too, brother,' Pushkara said, staring at the frightened eyes of Hemanga. 'Let us cook him.'

'Leave him,' Nala commanded. Reluctantly, Pushkara placed the swan down and took a few steps back. Hemanga lay wheezing on the cold floor. He could see the king limping towards him. The burn had turned to a boil on his toe and Hemanga felt sorry for what he had caused. Nala leaned before Hemanga and caressed his feathers.

'My brother says you can speak the human tongue. Can you?' Hemanga could feel the heat of Pushkara's stare on his feathers and decided it was prudent to keep quiet.

'Poor thing is hungry. Here, have it.' Nala picked a sweet and thrust it at Hemanga. The bird's eyes filled up. The swan wanted to say the sweet was not for him but for someone who would one day love Nala as her own. But he did not want to risk talking, especially with Pushkara around. He picked up the sweet and flew to the hole in the roof. He heard Nala saying, 'The poor mother is taking it to feed her babies.'

'It is a male,' Pushkara remarked acidly.

'Well, then a poor father is going to feed his babies,' Nala said with a smile and Pushkara turned on his heels to hurry out. Elated, Hemanga flew back to Vidarbha. He would present this as the token of love from Nala to Damayanti.

* * *

'I am not going to fly all the way to the kingdoms of barbarians to bring you more sweets, lady,' the swan quacked as it sauntered through the gardens. Since Damayanti had tasted Nala's sweet, things had turned out good for the bird. Now it was the princess who chased the bird and Hemanga enjoyed every bit of it. *Who knew a sweet would do such magic!* Being the messenger of love was not a bad idea, after all.

'He made such a wonderful present for you and what do you give Nala in return?' bickered the bird, 'Nothing?' Hemanga had not told her that Nala did not even know of her existence.

'I don't know how to cook,' Damayanti said with a sheepish smile.

'Hello, I am a messenger of love and not a transporter of food, young lady. So don't even think of it.'

'If you bring one sweet from him, I may let you sing,' the beautiful princess said, artfully.

'Aha, bribing, aren't we?'

'My sweet Hemanga, my bird of paradise, forget the sweet. Just tell me more about him,' sighed Damayanti.

'Who? Sage Narada? He keeps chanting Narayana, Narayana . . . Ouch, that hurt, young lady,' said the bird with mock severity.

'Fool,' she hissed.

'Fool, I am a fool? Audacious. Atrocious. A human calling a bird fool. Haah! What an irony,' remarked Hemanga. 'Devi, I was swimming in the sweet cold waters of the pond, looking for a delicious snack, a fish or a worm, and you summon me as if I am your slave! Imagine being disturbed during your meal. A meal is a meal whether you are a bird or a princess of an ancient kingdom. In Brahma Loka, there was this Gandharva . . . '

'Aren't you my friend?' Damayanti said in a voice dripping with honey. If she did not pacify the bird, he was sure to go on and on.

The swan hopped on to a rock and spread its wings to the sun. A golden feather got free and floated in the breeze. Damayanti caught it and a smile lit her face.

'Dreaming about the Nishada?' the swan asked, cocking his sinuous neck and squinting at her.

Damayanti sighed, 'You should have never talked about him.'

'Haah! So now it is my fault, Devi?' Hemanga asked. 'I am a connoisseur of beauty, young lady. There is so much beauty in the world that I can barely breathe. So, when I saw a man perfect as Nala, I was enchanted. When I am enchanted, I feel like singing. Now I am enchanted with your beauty. May I sing?'

'No!' Damayanti pouted.

'I will sing about him,' the swan said in a scheming voice.

'You are a swan, not a cuckoo. I have told you many times I don't want to suffer another horrendous song of yours.' Damayanti softened her remark with a smile, 'You can talk about him now, though.'

'That is an insult to my art and my sense of aesthetics. You don't deserve him, lady. You are mean and selfish. A spoiled rich woman and I am going to sing what a horrendous person you are.'

Damayanti swooped suddenly and caught the swan swiftly by his neck. 'No. I don't think so,' she said. 'You are going to *tell* me about him. Let me hear how handsome he is. What is the colour of his eyes? What is . . . '

The swan pecked her fingers and she let out a scream of pain. The bird flew away laughing hysterically.

'I hate you!' Damayanti screamed. 'If I see you again, I will catch you and take you to the kitchen. The cook will strip you off all those beautiful feathers and chop you into pieces and fry you!'

After taking an elegant arc in the sky, the swan perched on a branch above her, out of her reach. Then taking all its time, knowing fully well that the utterly beautiful princess' eyes were on him, it preened its feathers, slowly. When it was clear that the princess would stalk off in rage, the bird sweetly asked, 'Do you want to hear the song I made about Nala's cooking?'

Damayanti nodded, knowing well that no force in the world could stop the swan from singing now.

'Are you ready?' the swan asked with a mischievous twinkle in his eyes. Damayanti braced for the song. In a screechy voice the bird sang the praises of Nala, the Nishada king. Yet it transported her. She felt the world dissolve into sunlight that dripped through the canopy. A gentle breeze carrying the fragrance of kadamba flowers played with her honey skin. She felt it was his fingers that caressed her. Clouds swirled in the azure spring sky, forming the contours of Nala's face. Damayanti knew it was insane to fall in love with a man who she had never even seen. Such things only happened in fairy tales. Such love was impossible, she had thought, until it happened to her. Who would even believe that love was so painfully sweet and tortuous yet exhilarating, unless one has been struck by the flower arrow of Kama, the God of love? Unless one has not felt the heart longing with the pangs of separation, who would ever believe mango blossoms hid poetry in them?

'I shall go to the Nishada country on one condition,' Hemanga said, speaking the unspoken, and Damayanti's face brightened.

'But you need to give a token of love for Nala,' Hemanga said.

'I am not in love,' Damayanti pouted.

'Ok, Devi. My dinner is waiting in the pond. I had seen this big toad and he looked delicious.'

'Alright, alright. Would you take my poem to him?'

'A love poetry,' the swan sighed. 'How romantic.'

'It isn't a love poetry. It is just a poem about the moon.'

'Moon. How romantic!'

'Shut up and take this to him.'

The bird then replied pompously, 'I will think about it once I hear it.'

When Damayanti finished scribbling the couplet on a lotus leaf with the ink of hibiscus flowers, Hemanga took evil pleasure in making her read it aloud. Then he made her plead some more before flying to the Nishada country with it. Despite his tall claims, the golden swan had never met Nala after his brave adventure of stealing the sweet from Nala's kitchen and he still had no idea how he was going to convince Nala to marry Damayanti.

5

Poetry of Love

'Ah, poor hungry bird,' Nala said, as he placed a morsel of food before Hemanga. The bird picked up the savoury, while discreetly dropping the lotus leaf on which Damayanti had written the couplet. He flew out through the kitchen window and perched on the roof. Then he cautiously peered down through the hole, and his heart soared when he saw Nala picking up the lotus leaf. Hemanga held his breath as Nala started reading it. He watched Nala's face break into a smile.

The Nishada started humming the couplet. A dreamy look came to his eyes and Damayanti's words came alive in his mellifluous voice, as soothing as the southern breeze. Hemanga closed his eyes and listened.

The bird's heart melted in its melody. Damayanti's words and Nala's voice merged like moonlight and Nishagandhi flowers.

Nala did not know who wrote those lines, but it did not matter. For a connoisseur of art, the starting point of a brook or the destination of clouds floating away has always been irrelevant. The destination of the winding country path of a brook was of no relevance either. They loved beauty for its own sake. Such men became one with what they perceived and then they became no one. Nothing. They existed in the flit of the moment, throbbing with life, immortal, eternal.

Nala had finished singing. Hemanga sat drenched in its blissful shower, with his eyes closed. A gentle smoke curled up the roof, carrying the aroma of spices. Such was Nala's ecstasy while he was singing the song that Hemanga decided it was the right time to tell him about Damayanti.

He flew into the kitchen and whispered in Nala's ears, 'That song was written by someone in love.'

The bird's voice startled Nala from his reverie.

'Your Highness, I'm Hemanga, the messenger of love from Brahma Lok. Your brother is right. I can speak and I can even sing.' With that, Hemanga plunged into a breathless description of Damayanti, the Princess of Vidarbha, and her virtues.

'She is in love with you, Nala,' the golden swan finished and took a deep breath. He waited anxiously for Nala's reply.

The Nishada king shook his head dismissively. Hemanga felt his heart would break. 'She is your woman,' the swan said as if that statement would persuade Nala.

The Nishada king stood up and moved to the window. Outside, the sky looked like a purple silk sheet.

'I am a Nishada,' Nala said softly. For some time, the only sound was the drone of the crickets from the garden.

'Yes, you are the King of the Nishadas. And she is the Princess of Vidarbha. In love, all that matters is love,' the swan said with a sigh.

Nala turned towards the bird, 'My dear bird from Brahma Lok, perhaps in your world this does not matter. Here, in this holy land, all that matters is one's birth. And I am born in the wrong caste. She is far above my status. I am just a Nishada. The ways of humans are inferior to those of beasts. I would not even allow my mind to aspire for a woman like Damayanti. It would only lead to sorrow. Go and tell Damayanti the high born that she should forget this Nishada,' he said with great sorrow in his voice as he gently gathered and pushed Hemanga to the window.

'Strange is your world, Nala. For the creator, from the little worm to the mighty whale or from asuras to the King of Gods, Indra, all are equal. All of us are his children.'

'The Gods created by some drunken poets of the ancient times are more powerful here,' said Nala, his eyes bright. 'Such Gods have relevance only in the unhappiness of humans. In our world, golden bird, it is not the rule of the Brahma that reigns but the rules written by some hallucinating philosopher. They offer us the temptation of a heaven filled wine and doe-eyed damsels, and scare us with the visions of hell. Or they tempt us with a better life in our next birth. As a Nishada, if I obey all the scriptures, my reward would be to be born in a higher-caste womb the next life. By loving me—someone born in the womb of a forest dweller—the princess will only invoke the wrath of Gods. So go forth and tell your princess that she should marry someone noble and of her class.'

Nala gently pushed the bird out of the kitchen window and closed it. Hemanga pecked the windowpane, beseeching Nala to listen to him but the window remained shut.

Hemanga's tantrums brought Prince Pushkara out of his sleeping quarters. The swan knew soon the twin brother would have half of the Nishada country baying for his blood and chasing him with catapults and arrows. So he flew into the night with a heavy heart.

From the top of the temple flag mast, the cobra watched him fly away. The cobra then morphed into a bat and followed Hemanga.

6

Invitation

The next two months were excruciating for Hemanga. He had never indulged in such duplicity. He made many sorties about the Nishada kingdom and Vidarbha. He carried many couplets written by Damayanti and flew exotic dishes from Nala's kitchen. He watched Nala trying hard not to read Damayanti's poem and failing every time to resist the temptation. As for Damayanti, the princess never knew Nala's rejection of her. Hemanga never told her. The bird was worried to death. Every time he saw Damayanti's bliss, his guilt surged up. Yet he did not have the courage to tell Damayanti the truth. What truth he would say anyway, for he was sure Nala loved her dearly. It was apparent in the way Nala waited for Hemanga's arrival, and the way he soulfully sang the couplets written by Damayanti were proof enough of his love for her. Yet, he lived in a world in which he felt he was inadequate and as Hemanga understood more about humans, he could understand Nala's reluctance.

But it was Hemanga who had led them into this. They had not even heard about each other before they met him. He wished he could tell them that the human race actually depended on them, their love. That only if their love was true would humans escape total annihilation. But Brahma had forbidden him from telling anyone the reason for his visit to earth. Hemanga had to show that love between two humans was deep, true and would withstand, for the sake of love itself and not as a sacrifice for saving others. That was the only thing that would change the Brahma's mind. Their love must be selfish and selfless at the same time. Selfish, so that they love each other for the sake of themselves and not for some external motives and selfless, so that each is ready to sacrifice for the other. Hemanga kept praying fervently, wishing for a miracle.

Soon, a miracle did happen, but not in the way he had expected.

* * *

One day, the bird was flying over the Vidarbha city and was astonished to see the city decorated with festoons. Garlands of jasmine and hibiscus flowers adorned every lamp post. Workers were busy applying a fresh coat of lime to the walls. Mahouts atop elephants were spraying water on the royal path to settle the dust. Bards, street magicians, acrobat artists, palmists, and musicians were hurrying around on to the road. Shops selling condiments lined up the streets and the aroma of frying yams, bananas, and all sorts of savouries crowded the air.

Hemanga landed on the windowsill of Damayanti. She was sitting before the mirror and trying her ornaments.

'Hemanga!' Damayanti hugged him and pressed her cheek to his face. 'Where were you? My swayamvara is fixed.'

'Congratulations,' he said dryly, thinking how easily she had forgotten Nala.

'Oh, how wonderful! I never thought father would agree. All the ministers and the Rajguru were against it but King Bhimasena said that if it is a swayamvara, the bride's choice must be respected. Father has sent an invitation to Nala. Oh, how excited I am!'

'Devi,' Hemanga's voice was hoarse. He looked away, averting his eyes, and said, 'he won't come.'

She stared at him. 'What do you mean? Why won't he come?'

'Because he thinks he is not worthy of you. He is a lowly Nishada . . . '

'Father has sent him an invitation.'

'He won't come.'

Hemanga related Nala's words. Damayanti staggered to her bed and sat there with her eyes closed. Hemanga noticed a drop of tear grazing down her cheek and felt the heavy burden of guilt crushing his heart. *I have led her to this.* He was at a loss for words.

Then she stood up suddenly and hurried out of the room.

'Don't, please don't do anything stupid. He doesn't deserve you. Please!' Hemanga hopped hurriedly out of the room. A tide of panic threatened to overwhelm him. Among swans, the separation between loved ones meant the death of both. There were no widows or widowers among his tribe. Love was for this life and beyond; for eternity. *Where has she gone?* Hemanga went from room to room calling out her name. He burst into a room and found her staring at a birch leaf canvas.

'You scared me to death,' Hemanga panted. He watched her dip the peacock feather tip in ink and draw on the canvas. Soon, Nala was peering lovingly into the half-closed eyes of Damayanti.

On the canvas, a full moon peeped coyly through the leaves. Like a creeper entwining a tree, Damayanti was wrapped in Nala's arms. Behind them, there was a gentle cascade, and even a golden swan in the pond. Damayanti finished her final touches and stepped back to admire her work.

'Exquisite! Perfect,' the swan crooned. 'I should make a poem about the two of you and sing it at your wedding.'

'Before the sun turns to the colour of a ripened mango tomorrow, you will fly south carrying my gift to him. Tell him Damayanti is waiting for him,' Damayanti commanded, rolling the canvas and tying it with a string of pearls. Hemanga took it and bowed.

If the painting did not convince Nala that he was meant to be the husband of Damayanti, nothing else would, thought Hemanga as he flew to the Nishada country.

7

The Three Gods

Hemanga was drinking water from a forest brook when he heard a twig breaking. The painting was secured on the shore with a stone. A gush of wind made the scroll flutter and Hemanga eyed it with concern. The swan dipped its beak for another gulp of water when a sudden wind knocked him off his feet. Cursing and spluttering, the swan was on its feet when it saw a terrifying sight. The scroll was rolling away bouncing, arching around bushes, now getting caught in shrubs, only to be blown farther and farther up the hills.

'Oh, no, no, stop. Where are you going? Don't make me run like this. Come back, you stupid painting,' Hemanga screeched as he gave chase to the fast-rolling scroll. A hare darted across Hemanga's path, forcing him to halt. The scroll shot up, rising higher and higher. That's when Hemanga noticed what was strange: not a leaf or blade of grass steered, there was no breeze, yet the scroll was flying away.

'This is foul play. Some devil is trying to play pranks. I will show who I am,' muttered Hemanga under his breath, face puffing with anger. He then ran faster to chase the scroll with renewed vigour. Halfway through the chase, it dawned on him that he was being utterly stupid. 'I am a swan. Why am I running like a dog after a cat?'

So he took off to catch the scroll that was flitting in the air like a kite cut loose from its string. He almost got it between his beak when it was suddenly snatched away. It hovered before his eyes tantalizingly within his reach. Hemanga yanked at it and it was pulled back again.

'Devils, Asuras, Rakshasas, who are you? Come out in the open and fight me,' Hemanga screamed. He repeated his abuse in all tongues he knew. Someone was making fun of him. The scroll was within his reach, but never in his grasp. Suddenly he felt a sting on the back of his neck. Yelping, he turned and saw three figures standing before him. They weren't standing exactly, for there was a gap of a few fingers between their feet and the ground—practically levitating. Though the afternoon sun blazed above, they had no shadows and Hemanga could see through them, all the way to the distant river as if they were made of thin air.

'Wh . . . wh . . . who are you?' stuttered Hemanga. He had challenged to fight them but now, he was not sure of the wisdom of his challenge.

Then the one with the complexion of dark night snatched the hovering painting from the air and unfolded it.

'Hey, hey, hey!' protested Hemanga. 'That is most uncivil; haven't your parents taught you any manners? It is not meant for you.' They ignored the swan and continued to stare at the painting.

The second one who had the complexion of silver, said, 'More beautiful than any Apsara in my abode.'

The third one with the translucent, burning copper-complexion, the one whose mere touch had scathed Hemanga's feathers, uttered with scorn, 'To think that she is in love with a lowly Nishada!'

The dark-complexioned one grunted. Scratching his chin he said, 'She is a treasure to be cherished.'

'Atrocious!' Hemanga was livid. He added, 'To pass such a comment on a lady! Shame on you.'

Then he tried to peck them with his beak. Just then, the silver-complexioned one slapped the bird with the back of his hand and the force of it flung Hemanga over the hill. He lay wheezing, stunned at the power of the blow for a few moments. Then he came back.

'I am the swan of Brahma's world. I can't stand disrespect to a woman. I will kill you.' He screamed.

There they were, the scoundrels, sitting around the painting, looking at Damayanti with evil eyes. The bird dove at them and was stopped short by the grip of the copper-hued one. Hemanga's throat started burning. He could smell his own smouldering flesh. The copper-skinned one's eyes glowered with intensity. The swan used the last of his will to glower back at him. If he was going to die, which he was sure now, he would not do it with his head bent in fear. With what little strength he could muster, he decided to fight. He pecked with all his might on the wrist of the hand that was holding his throat. Both yelled in pain together and the grip loosened from Hemanga's throat. Hemanga found his beak was on fire where it had touched the copper-hued one's skin. His companions laughed aloud.

'Agni, the God of fire, bested by a little swan,' the silver-skinned one howled with laughter. Hemanga rubbed his smouldering beak on the grass, moaning with pain, when he processed the words and stopped short. *These were no asuras.* The silver-skinned one then knelt before Hemanga, 'we are pleased with your devotion to the one you serve,' he said, gently touching Hemanga's beak. The pain vanished.

'Who . . . who are you?' Hemanga asked.

'I am Indra, the King of Gods,' the silver-skinned one said, 'and the one you pecked is Agnideva, the God of fire. The dark-skinned one is Yama, the God of death.'

Hemanga shuddered. The God of death was looking at him with interest.

'You . . . you are not real. You are the creatures of imagination, sprung in some poet's brain,' Hemanga stuttered.

'So are you. So is everyone. What makes you think that we all are not transient beings in the dream of Brahma,' smiled Indra.

'And what if that Brahma himself is the imagination of a super Brahma?' asked Yama.

'And what if this super Brahma is nothing but a dream of a superior Brahma who himself is a dream of superlative Brahma and so on?' asked Agni.

'There is no truth,' offered Indra.

'There are only true lies,' pronounced Agni.

'. . . and real illusions,' added Yama helpfully.

Hemanga felt his head would burst. It was all so confusing. 'You are drunk with Soma,' Hemanga said, more to satisfy his urge for a comeback than to make any sense. Nothing made sense anymore. His comment made the Gods laugh aloud. Maybe they are not as evil as he thought, he told himself, though they definitely lacked good breeding. They were joking with each other. Hemanga eyed the painting lying on the grass. This was his chance to get rid of these boors. The bird quietly stretched his neck and was about to grasp the scroll when Yama pressed his foot on it.

'Sly, aren't we?' he grinned showing his impossibly white teeth. He had a deadly smile. Hemanga shuddered at the sight.

Indra picked Hemanga by his neck and said not unkindly, 'What is your dharma, my swan?'

'I . . . I am the messenger of love,' Hemanga squeaked.

'Then, be our messenger of love. Fly back and tell the beautiful Damayanti to choose one among us as her husband,' said Indira dreamily, sighing at the painting.

'I am in love with her,' Yama said.

'So am I,' Agni agreed.

'Tell the princess to forget that low-caste Nishada. Tell her that the immortal Gods are waiting for her hand,' Indra said, gently placing the swan down, 'Go, bird of love. Sing our poem of passion to the princess.'

'Never!' The shrillness of his voice surprised Hemanga himself. 'Nala and Damayanti are made for each other,' he said, adding, 'There is no love purer than this.'

The three Gods burst out in laughter. 'There is nothing like pure love,' Indra said trying hard to control his mirth.

'What do you know about love?' Hemanga contested haughtily. 'You have a thousand wives and countless apsaras as your mistresses.' He then turned to Agni and said, 'and who would marry you, God of fire? You eat everything without discretion. You love nothing but lust over everything. You swallow what you see, leaving behind only ashes. Why should a woman care for you?'

Yama laughed loudly. Hemanga spun towards him with a flash of anger, 'And you, the God of death, the joker among Gods, the fool who comes bequeathed and unwanted . . . you render everything meaningless. Everyone hates you.'

Hemanga who used his words like darts aimed to hurt and provoke, was instead left surprised. The Gods laughed raucously with each of his pronouncements, hurling the insults that Hemanga had said at each other. They laughed like drunken hooligans in a tavern, slapping each other's backs.

Hemanga rolled his eyes. These Gods were disgusting. Between his laughter, Indra said, 'You are a naive messenger of love. The Nishada, hopefully, will be wiser. Take us to him and we shall convince him that he is unworthy of Damayanti.

That suck away Hemanga's breath. He could feel a weight on his chest. The Nishada king had already expressed his sense of inadequacy, and his fear of inferiority. The painting that Damayanti drew was to convince him that he was in no way inferior and was the worthiest man for her. Now the Gods were asking Hemanga to deepen the sense of fear and inferiority that the Nishada king harboured due to the accident of his birth in a low caste.

'I can't,' Hemanga said.

'You can't or you won't?' Indra cocked an eyebrow and looked at the bird.

'I won't, I won't, I won't,' Hemanga said defiantly as if repeating it thrice would make the three Gods go away. The trio burst out laughing again. The next moment they were hurling through the sky at a breakneck speed. Hemanga gasped for breath as the clouds whizzed under them. Then, the earth curved below him in a nerve-racking velocity. Indra was holding him by his legs and Hemanga was hanging upside down, flaying his wings in a desperate attempt to escape.

'You are so entertaining, little swan. I think a position in my court as the jester would suit you,' said Indra as they crossed a row of low hills and curved around a river. The wind gushed past Hemanga's ears and the smart retort he uttered in response to Indra's request came garbled. The Gods continued to laugh for no reason. Hemanga could see the vast jungle and the city of the Nishadas at the centre of it approaching. When they reached there, they flew past the towering temple towers, swirled around the palace turret, and went around the palace bell tower thrice. Yama flew towards the palace bell and started clanging it furiously. When the soldiers ran out in alarm, the three Gods circumvented the palace at lightning speed in search of Nala's room.

* * *

Prince Pushkara was leading the soldiers in the courtyard. Hemanga saw the prince pointing at him. 'It is that blasted talking swan.'

'He is flying upside down,' cried a soldier.

'Just to make me mad. Shoot the devil down,' yelled Pushkara and the archers drew their bows. Hemanga sputtered in rage, 'Fools, can't you see I am a hostage!?'

'They can't see us, only you,' Yama whispered in Hemanga's ears.

'You will rot in hell, you imbecile!' Hemanga yelled at Yama, the God of death.

'He owns hell,' said Indra and the three Gods howled in laughter.

From the courtyard, Pushkara screamed, 'Now the talking bird is hurling abuses. How dare he curse me to rot in hell? Kill him. *Now*!'

'You fool, I did not abuse you, you idiot,' Hemanga cried as the Gods made him fly past an inch above Pushkara's head, knocking his headgear down.

'Now you did just that, little swan. You called him a fool and an idiot. And *you* knocked down his headgear. Look! He is not pleased about it,' Indra winked at him.

'If they start shooting, you too will die,' Hemanga said.

Pushkara trembled with rage, 'Now he wants me to die.'

Hemanga said, 'Oh no, I didn't mean you.' The Gods howled with laughter.

'The devil is laughing at me after wishing me death,' cried Pushkara. 'Shoot him down!' an infuriated Pushkara commanded.

Soon the arrows started whizzing past and the bird screamed in terror. 'Stop, stop. Are you crazy?' The Gods were having the time of their lives. They flew in circles, doing impossible manoeuvres, evading the arrows and stones that the Nishadas shot at Hemanga.

'Mocking me and humiliating me?! None of your aerial stunts is going to save you,' Pushkara screamed back. Hemanga was being hurled around, now flying sideways, now upside down, now spiralling down and then shooting straight up. The more the invisible Gods did aerial stunts, the more agitated and angrier the Nishadas got. Hearing the commotion in the palace courtyard, King Nala opened the window of his chamber.

'What is it, Pushkara?' Nala asked. The next moment, the three Gods dove right into Nala's chamber and dropped Hemanga at the feet of Nala.

'Hemanga?' Nala was surprised. Hemanga struggled to get his breath back. From the courtyard, Pushkara yelled, 'Brother, do not let that demon bird escape. I am coming there and going to tear that infernal swan from limb to limb!'

'Gods . . . Gods, three of them,' Hemanga gasped, 'they made me do this. They . . . ' Hemanga's voice trailed as he saw Nala picking up the scroll. The Nishada king stared at the picture that Damayanti had drawn for a moment. Hemanga saw Nala's eyes sparkling with tears. At that moment he knew no Gods would ever be able to persuade Nala to forget Damayanti. Hemanga looked triumphantly at the Gods standing in the corner. The Gods had not made themselves visible to him. Then Yama winked at Hemanga and blood raged in the swan's wings.

'Nala,' Indra called, startling Nala from his reverie. The three Gods appeared like apparitions and Nala staggered back in shock. The painting fell from his hand.

'I am Indra, the King of Gods, this is Agni, the God of fire, and Yama, the God of death,' he said.

Nala bowed reverently and Hemanga knew what the Gods were trying: they were going to use Nala's noble nature against him.

'It is an honour that you have chosen to appear before a humble Nishada,' Nala said.

'I know you are a noble soul and value your word.'

'Word? What word? He has given you no word, you devious, wily, sly Gods,' Hemanga cried from the floor. The Gods ignored him. Indra took Nala's hands and pressed them to his chest, 'We wish to marry Damayanti.'

'No, don't worry,' Agni added quickly with a chuckle, 'she won't have three husbands.'

Indra said, 'We need you to convince her to choose one among us.'

Nala's face darkened.

'I am sure you would keep your word, Nala,' Yama grinned.

'They are manipulating you,' Hemanga cried as he saw the hesitation in Nala's face.

'Do you really think the noble and high-born Princess of Vidarbha would marry a Nishada?' Indra asked.

'You will be ridiculed, Nala, if you go to the swayamvara and well . . . er . . . get ignored,' Agni added.

'Think about it. You are a noble soul, Nala. You are the leader of your tribe. Imagine you coming back humiliated and people laughing behind your back. The bards would be entertaining the people of Aryavartha with the tales of the

Nishada who fell for the prank of a mischievous princess,'
Indra said.

'Whom you have not seen even once,' Agni added helpfully.

'She deserves one of us, the immortals. If you love her,
which we are sure you do, you should do what is best for her,'
Yama said.

'Isn't that what love is all about? Selfless and all that,' Indra
smiled charmingly.

'Would your people accept her? Would she be happy here
in this Nishada kingdom?' Agni said.

'Nala, why do you want to humiliate yourself? Convince
Damayanti to marry one of us,' Indra said with a benevolent
smile. Hemanga saw indecision, fear, insecurity, and his sense
of inferiority—all parade in succession through Nala's face.
Hemanga's heart sank. He had thought Nala was the perfect
man for the perfect woman. *This man didn't have the courage of
conviction for standing up for his love.*

'How . . . how will I convince her? I will be meeting her
only at the time of the swayamvara and it won't be possible
to persuade her in that short time, that too fully in the view
of all other guests,' Nala said in a low voice. Hemanga felt all
his efforts had gone in vain. *Was it for such a meek man he had
risked his life?* As he watched Nala's struggles with his sense of
inferiority, Hemanga understood it wasn't the Gods that Nala
feared, but himself. *He was inviting Kali to his life.*

'You don't deserve her, Nala,' Hemanga cried out, 'if you
are going to tell her to marry someone else.'

'You are right,' Nala mumbled.

'Good advice,' Indra patted Hemanga. Indra took out a ring
from the folds of his waistcloth and offered it to Nala, 'Nala, this
is the ring of invisibility. We immortals do not need it as we

know how to be visible or invisible at our will, but for you, this would come in handy.'

Nala stood staring at the dark ring that shimmered in Indra's palm. Hemanga wished Nala would come to his senses and fling the ring of invisibility through the window. He saw Nala taking it with trembling hands and the three Gods stood watching with sly smiles on their lips.

'Don't sell your love, don't pawn your soul,' Hemanga pleaded. Nala twirled the black ring between his thumb and index fingers and with a faraway look, said, 'Gods, you have been kind to this Nishada. I would have done it even without these blessings, for Damayanti is far above my stature. I am not good enough for her.' And with that, Nala turned around and left.

'You have tricked him, you villains,' Hemanga cried out in grief and anger.

'And there goes your true love,' Yama snickered.

Hemanga rummaged his brain to give a stinging retort. Finally, he came up with something. 'You are a cunning, sleazy, manipulative scoundrel!' spat Hemanga, but immediately found himself staring at the enraged face of Pushkara. The Gods had vanished leaving him to his fate, and the abuse he had meant for the Gods had found its mark on Pushkara.

'Abusive as usual, eh?' Pushkara hissed and drew his sword from his scabbard.

'No, no, no,' Hemanga screamed running from one corner of the room to another for his dear life as Pushkara swung his sword to decapitate Hemanga's head.

'Say your prayers, bird,' Pushkara yelled. Footsteps thundered through the stairs. More Nishadas were coming into the room to slaughter Hemanga.

'I didn't mean you,' Hemanga cried as Pushkara's sword swiped a feather off his tail. 'Argh! Easy, easy. I meant the immortals, you fool!'

'What do you mean by immortals?' Pushkara advanced menacingly, gripping his sword tight.

'The ones who don't die, not you though. You will die for sure,' Hemanga said. Pushkara paused 'What did you just say?'

'Oh, oh, oh . . . no, no, no, no . . . I didn't mean you would die now . . . but you would die for sure,' Hemanga gulped, 'one day . . .'

Silence.

'Er . . . I think that came all wrong,' Hemanga said, trying to walk backward and away from the advancing Pushkara. 'Let me try to explain.' He hit the walls and could go no further.

'You are the one who is going to die now,' Pushkara yelled and rushed towards Hemanga. Just then, a flash of lightning, followed by an ear-splitting roll of thunder shook the entire palace. Shell-shocked, Pushkara turned back and saw that the curtains behind him had caught fire.

Nishadas were jostling to get into the room to butcher Hemanga, but when they saw the fire, most of them turned on their heels and fled. They collided with those rushing up the stairs and knocked them over. Amid this turmoil, Hemanga escaped.

* * *

As he was flying back to Vidarbha, Hemanga vowed that he would not give up. If the man were not man enough to face his own fears and inadequacy, maybe the woman would be woman enough to stand up against the Gods. It was in Damayanti he should trust, he decided.

Damayanti was waiting anxiously for Nala to appear. The night had grown old and the most of decorative lamps that lined the fort walls, balconies, and the city streets had died down. Here and there, like eyes of some strange beasts, a few lamps flickered.

8

The Meeting

'How dare he give such a word after writing me such a tender poem, after sending me such delicious treats, after filling my dreams with sweetness, how dare he even think of leaving me! Let him come here and I will give him an earful,' Damayanti was furious when Hemanga told her everything.

'Easy, lady, easy. Please be kind to him.'

'Kind to him!' Damayanti said, her eyes sparkling with unshed tears. 'Bah! Kind to him indeed, I am going to make him regret every word he spoke to those Gods. Gods indeed. Nothing more than a miserable mischievous gang of troublemakers. To think that they want to marry me! The audacity of it. The atrociousness of it. And you say Nala agreed to help them. Help them! I am waiting to meet Nala.'

'Devi, this is your first meeting,' the bird hastened to calm the feisty princess. 'Be sweet to him, cajole him. Give him confidence, express your love tenderly, and maybe even sing a song. Haven't you heard how it happens in the stories that the bards croon.'

'Bah! Let him come here, this is no fairy tale, I will show him the real Damayanti. I will give him a mouthful.'

'You will frighten him away, lady. With this temper of yours, even I wonder if you would be better off marrying that fire God or death God. Or Indra, the lord of thunder.'

'Yama, Agni, Indra . . . I am waiting to meet them, as well. I will wring their necks and murder them.'

'You can't,' Hemanga said.

'What do you mean by I can't? Watch me doing it.'

'They are immortals, they can't die.'

'Well, then they are going to regret that they were ever born when they meet me and pray for their deaths.'

'They weren't born. Brahma created them,' Hemanga contested hotly.

'Would you please keep quiet? I have no time to argue.'

'Oh! So now it is my fault?'

'Yes! It is all your fault. You came with the message of love. I was living happily and there comes a talking bird. The know-all birdie. A thief who steals sweets from someone's kitchen and ruins my life.'

'I didn't steal. Nala gave it to me,' Hemanga said indignantly.

'Nala, Nala . . . why doesn't he come?' Damayanti cried.

'I am here,' a voice came from nowhere and Damayanti screamed in terror.

'It is him,' Hemanga whispered.

'Where, where are you,' Damayanti asked, looking behind the curtains, looking around here and looking around there.

'I am here, Devi,' Nala appeared behind her as he removed the ring of invisibility from his fingers. For a moment Damayanti stared at him and her eyes filled up. Nala looked away, unable to face her, and the next moment, she was hugging him, sobbing on his shoulders. He stood stunned, moved by her action, not knowing how to say what he had come to say.

'You want me to forget you, Nala?' Damayanti asked Nala, who sat on the cot, looking down. She sat beside him and took his arm.

'I . . . I am a Nishada, I am not worthy of . . . ' the words broke as Damayanti kissed him fully on his lips. Hemanga's chest swelled with pride. No Gods were going to break this love, no force was going to part them. He sneaked out of the bedroom and flew out through the window, leaving the lovers to be with each other.

Hemanga flew higher and higher, shrieking with joy and did a spiral dive, crying, 'Indra, Yama and Agni—the three idiots . . . *whoopee!* You lost.' The faces of the three Gods hovered around him as he hurtled down to earth. One by one, each face broke into a hideous smile and a tremor of fear ran down the spine of the bird of love. The Gods were planning something mischievous.

9

Swayamvara

Hemanga was stuck to the top of a pillar. *The Gods' infernal trick*, the swan fumed. He could see the princes arriving for Damayanti's swayamvara. King Bhimasena welcomed each of them warmly and led them to their designated seats.

An uncomfortable hush fell, and all heads turned to the door. Nala, the King of Nishadas, walked into the hall and a low murmur rose. 'How dare a Nishada be among us,' the murmuring grew louder. King Bhimasena recovered quickly and gestured to his courtiers to welcome the Nishada.

Nala stood embarrassed, blushing dark, becoming keenly aware of the snub he had received. King Bhimasena moved forward, grasped Nishada's hand, and took him to the seat reserved for him. The princes who sat on either side of the empty seat excused themselves and moved a few seats away.

Bhimasena looked pleadingly at the chief priest sitting cross-legged before the holy altar. The chief priest shook his head slowly from side to side. Bhimasena hurried to convince him when a commotion arose in the hall. Nala jumped to his feet. His gaze was fixed at the door and his expression looked as if he had seen a ghost.

The man at the door walked in and people stared at him in shock. He bowed to Nala and took one of the empty seats by his side. Hemanga gasped. The newcomer was a replica of Nala. Bhimasena hurried to the newcomer, confusion writ on his face. The king froze at his gait and stared at the entrance. Another Nala was walking in. The newcomer nonchalantly took a seat on the right side of the first Nala. Before the confusion died down, one more Nala appeared. He followed all the gestures of those who preceded him and took a seat near Nala. Now there were four Nalas sitting in a row, each a spitting image of the other. Hemanga was furious. He knew the three Gods had played an abominable trick. They have all taken the form of Nala to confuse Damayanti.

The conch blew for the princess's arrival. All eyes turned towards the inner door. Musicians played their flutes and mridangams. Auspicious music filled the air. Three maids entered carrying vases filled with exotic perfumes. They sprayed the perfume in the air with yak tail whiskers and a giddy aroma filled the hall. The princess sat breathless in anticipation. All eyes were on Damayanti and nobody could be blamed for not being able to take their eyes off her.

Looking even more beautiful than any apsara or goddess, decked in sparkling ornaments, wrapped in the finest of silks, dazzling everyone with her angelic smile, she stood there holding a garland of jasmine flowers. As she walked past, each king or prince rose to bow to her. She paused before each of them and graced them with a smile or a word of polite greeting, and then breaking their hearts, proceeded to the next suitor. The men who Damayanti rejected were not taking their humiliation lightly. Hemanga had heard tales about swayamvaras going awry and the winner of the maiden's hand hacked to death by the thwarted rivals and he grew worried.

Damayanti paused before the four Nalas. They stood up and bowed together as if they were all puppets controlled by the same string. 'Nala,' Damayanti whispered softly and they answered in unison, 'Devi, at your service.'

Hemanga wondered how was she going to get out of the confusion. Damayanti then sang two lines of a poem she had composed. Hemanga remembered it. It was the first poem of hers that expressed her love for him. It was a secret that only Damayanti, Nala, and Hemanga, the messenger of love knew. In reply, Nala had written and completed the quartet, which Hemanga had carried back to her.

'Now you are trapped,' Hemanga chuckled looking at the three impostors. Damayanti waited for Nala to reply. All the four Nalas sang together the second portion of the quartet. *How did the roguish Gods know the secret between the lovers!* The answer came to his mind in a trice. The Gods were reading Nala's mind. *All was lost.* Hemanga wanted to wail. Damayanti would choose the wrong Nala and she would be whisked away by the immortals to their world, the bird thought with a sinking heart.

Sunlight filtering through the roof tiles illuminated the four Nalas. People shifted their feet. Priests forgot to fan the embers in the sacrificial altar as they watched the drama unfolding. *There must be a way to distinguish mortals from immortals*, Damayanti thought in desperation. But nothing struck her. Time was running out.

'The *muhurta* will be coming to an end soon,' the chief priest's voice boomed, breaking the tense silence. Damayanti could hear the drops falling in the water clock rhythmically. Her forehead lined with perspiration. The four Nalas smiled at her.

Then she saw it. There were beads of sweat forming on the forehead of one Nala. The other three did not have it. They had either missed to imitate sweating or were not capable of it. She suppressed the joy that was bubbling up. She leaned forward and raised the garland, pausing for a moment before a

Nala who was not sweating. Yama bent his head for her to put the garland on his shoulder and choose him as her man. He did not know she tempted him only to confirm her doubts. She leaned over his shoulder and looked for shadows and, as she had guessed, only one of the four had a shadow—the same one who was sweating.

As the water clock dripped its last drop to the bowl indicating the time was up, Damayanti quickly turned and put the garland on her Nala's shoulders and enveloped him in a tight embrace. Everyone in the durbar rose. Damayanti sobbed on his shoulders. She had outwitted the Gods.

Damayanti did not hear the uproar her choice had caused. She did not see the kings and princes, men of noble castes, son of illustrious dynasties, warriors, and scholars yet mere men who had never learnt to respect the choice of women, rushing forward with their drawn swords to hack the Nishada to death. Hemanga saw the rush to finish off the lovers. Then there was a flash of light that stunned them in their tracks. Hemanga saw the three Gods assuming their original forms.

'Fools! Nala and Damayanti are now under our protection. Who dares to fight Indra?' the King of Gods thundered.

'And Agni,' raged the God of fire.

'And me,' said Yama, assuming his deadly form. The princes who were boasting about their valour some time before, scampered for their lives like a pack of mice before a hungry cat. The priests who were invoking the Gods with their sacred chants bolted when the Gods appeared for real. King Bhimasena alone stood in his place, tears streaming from his eyes. Indra took the hand of Nala and walked him to the king. Agni and Yama walked on either side of Damayanti. Hemanga found he was free of the Gods' curse and was no longer stuck to the pillar top. He flew down, shrieking with joy. 'The purity of love has won,' he cried. *Humankind has been saved*, Hemanga exulted. He flew around in the palace hall singing with joy.

'King Bhimasena, give the hand of your daughter to the one she loves,' Indra said with a smile. The king looked at the empty *mandap*, the priests had run away. They would now come back only when it was safe to collect their fees.

'Here is Agni, the God of fire, as witness to their union,' Indra said. King Bhimasena placed the hand of his daughter, who was uncharacteristically shy and coy, on the palm of the grateful Nala. Bhimasena's eyes brimmed with tears and with a shaky voice he said, 'You have more courage than any of those kings, my daughter. You were challenged by the Gods and you stood steadfast in love. Who am I to stand in your way? Which customs or traditions can dare to break your love? May you live for a hundred happy years together with the man of your choice. May you share joy and sorrow, triumphs and failures, good and ill health, by being dependable to each other. May you live a blessed life with a bit of sorrow that would sweeten the happiness and turn it to bliss. Go to the land of the Nishadas and make it more prosperous. Be the pillar of your husband's home, the spine of his life, the roof over his head. Once in a while, come home as your father's guest and help me relish the memories of my youth when you were a little bundle of joy, in my lap.'

Damayanti hugged her father tight and cried; Nala stood awkward, not sure of the social norm, unsure whether he was welcome in his illustrious father-in-law's home. The next moment King Bhimasena pulled the Nishada towards his bosom and blessed him, 'I am sure you would keep her happy. She has chosen well.'

Hemanga was moved to tears, he had never expected this to end up so well and so easily. The Gods had vanished. Hemanga looked around, feeling remorse: he ought to find them and seek their apology. He had misunderstood them. They had been merely testing the couple's love and were not in fact evil. He had uttered harsh words and even abused them; *he must apologize*. Once he would've done that and lightened his heart, he could then come back and say goodbye to the couple he had helped unite.

The thought of going home made Hemanga homesick. The thought of telling the tale of his adventures to his admiring friends brought a smile to his face.

* * *

Hemanga found them sitting by the side of the Narmada river. They had a cloth board of *dyuta* spread before them. Indra was shaking the cowrie shells in the cup of his hands when Hemanga landed near him.

In his happiness, Hemanga found himself babbling, 'I came to apologize, my Lords. You aren't as bad as I thought. Well, a bit mischievous and all . . . '

The Gods ignored him. Indra threw the cowrie shells and shouted, 'Thirty!'

When they stopped spinning, he cried in delight and moved one of his four pieces in an anti-clockwise direction. Then Agni started shaking the cowries in the cup of his palms.

'What are you doing?' Hemanga asked, peering into the board.

'Huh! We are dancing. Can't you see that?' Yama said.

'Ha ha,' Hemanga laughed, eager to please, 'this seems like a nice game. What is it called?'

'It is a game of fate. The fate of humans depends on how the cowrie shells fall,' Agni said. Hemanga felt a sudden chill. 'Ha ha,' he laughed nervously, 'how . . . how can three play a board game. Either it should be two or it should be four?'

'We are four,' Yama said, throwing the cowrie shells.

'Including me, four?' Hemanga laughed, 'but you are only three . . . '

Hemanga's words trailed to a whimper as he saw a terrifying sight. The cowrie shells rose in the air by themselves and rattled as if someone was shaking them inside the cup of his palm. The invisible hand flung the cowries on the floor with force. They rolled, spun, and stopped. Agni and Yama cursed. The coins on the board started moving by themselves.

'I . . . I . . . don't understand,' Hemanga stammered, backtracking, 'Good day, Gods. I . . . I . . . I came to say goodbye, see you. Bye.'

'Oh, you are giving up so easily?' Indra said, moving a coin.

'What . . . what do you mean?' Hemanga did not know where it was going but instinctively knowing this was not going somewhere pleasant. 'I have done my job. Great satisfaction, sir. It is a wonderful feeling. Ah, the pure, selfless love of the couple.'

The three Gods burst into laughter.

'Silence,' a voice snapped, startling Hemanga. The sinister shout made Hemanga's blood go cold. He slowly walked backwards, trying to calm his pounding heart. The game of dyuta was still on among the three Gods or . . . Was there a fourth one? He could sense an evil presence. There was poison in the air.

'I . . . I am leaving,' Hemanga stammered.

'Get lost,' a voice growled. The three Gods sat hunched over the game of dice.

'I will make him suffer. You had no business defending him,' the invisible voice hissed.

'We tested them, and they won. We can't be unfair,' Indra said softly.

A moment's silence followed. Hemanga could hear the wind rustling dry leaves. And the next moment the jungle exploded with an uproarious laughter. 'Tested? Hah . . . tested . . . dressing up like that Nishada was your way of testing? A four-year-old would have enjoyed such a silly game. Tested their love indeed.'

The three Gods looked uneasy.

'It is so easy for all of you, isn't it? You come here whenever you please, have your fun and go back. What about me? I am tied to the fortunes of humans. You are all created by Brahma. I am not. So, you think it is alright if I suffer?' The voice growled.

Silence reigned for a moment. Then the voice grumbled again, 'I am chained to earth, chained to human destiny. It would be a blessing if humans are wiped out as Brahma wants it. Then I could be free.' Without a word, the three Gods continued to play. And lose.

The air on the winner's side had started to thicken. Black smoke swirled, shifting its shape, thickening and thinning. As the terrified Hemanga watched, the smoke thickened to form a human shape. *Kali, the God of misfortune.* Hemanga staggered back. His head was reeling, throat going dry.

'I will show that low-life Nishada and his arrogant bride what it is to be tested by the real God. The only God. Kali!' The last word was uttered with so much force that the earth shook, and thunder clapped in the sky. A sudden gale bent the trees and swirled dust clouds and dry leaves in the air. The dark shadowy form of Kali throbbed. His fiery eyes glowered.

'Fool!' Kali roared, pointing his index finger at Hemanga. 'Messenger of love indeed! Bah! Daring to challenge Kali? I am the God who dwells in the darkest corners of the human mind. Fear is my food. And I am going to play dice with Nala and Damayanti's fate.' The dark God of misfortune roared with laughter.

Hemanga flew away, scared but determined. He should warn Nala and Damayanti. The laughter of Kali followed. When Hemanga reached the Nishada land, the wedding procession of Nala and Damayanti was entering the city of Nishadas. Pushkara waited at the gates to welcome his brother and sister-in-law.

When Pushkara saw Damayanti, a finger of fire traced its way down his dry throat and poked his heart. Had Pushkara turned and looked at his shadow, he could have seen Kali lurking in the darkness of it and leering at him.

Hemanga saw it and his heart sank.

10

Pushkara

It was eerily silent, the kind of noiselessness that made one's hair behind the neck stand erect. Hemanga looked around, trying to figure out the chamber of Nala. He thought he should warn the couple about the impending peril. After having ascertained the chamber of Nala and Damayanti, he rested on the branch of a Peepal tree that stood before the temple, watching over their window while the moon crawled up behind the temple tower, accentuating the smooth contours of its carvings with a thread of silver.

Hemanga was drooping into his sleep when a scrapping sound startled him. A man was crawling up the wall like a lizard towards the window of Nala's chamber. Hanging with one hand, the man took a folding knife from his waistband and opened it with his teeth. He furtively looked around. *Prince Pushkara! What was the brother of King Nala doing at this time of the night, hanging from the window of the king's bedroom? Murder!* Hemanga's mind screamed, but he was mute with fear. Pushkara prised open the window. Moonlight streamed inside and fell on Damayanti's face. The sudden chill might have made her stir in her sleep. She snuggled closer to her husband. For a long time, Pushkara hung watching from the window, the face of his sleeping sister-in-law, before he crawled back to his own window and disappeared into it.

Hemanga wanted an explanation for this strange behaviour of the prince. He peeped inside Pushkara's chamber through the crack in the window. The prince was sitting at the edge of his cot with his face buried in his palms.

'I am a sinner. I am evil,' Pushkara's voice broke as he rocked back and forth like a man possessed. He sprang up and started pacing up and down his room, mumbling incoherently. 'Why should my brother have it all? I am his twin; younger by only a few minutes. Yet he has the kingship, fame, and power. And now he has her. He has her! Damayanti's beautiful face is haunting me in my dreams.' He went on ranting for a while and then suddenly rushed towards the window. Hemanga fled just in time to not be noticed. But as he turned back mid-flight, he saw Pushkara crawling back again towards Nala's window.

The moon had now disappeared behind dark clouds. It was so dark that the slithering figure of Pushkara merged with the stone wall. Then Hemanga saw another figure crawling behind Pushkara. It was a shadow darker than the darkest of nights. As Pushkara once again peeped into his brother's chamber, the dark shadow that had followed him turned towards Hemanga and glared at him with its hollow eyes. Hemanga flew faster with his life.

Kali had begun his game.

A few days later, Hemanga finally managed to find Damayanti alone. She had finished her swimming and was sitting on the granite steps of the lotus pond. Damayanti was delighted to see him, but Hemanga had no time to waste. He warned her about Pushkara. Damayanti laughed, 'Yes, I too have noticed his roving eyes. When my back is turned, I can feel his lust burning my skin. But he is young and is devoted to his brother. He will grow out of it when he finds his own love, sooner or later. He is just a boy.'

Hemanga told her what he had witnessed, and she smiled, 'Oh! Is he now crawling on the stone walls like a lizard? You're dreaming, Hemanga. Don't you know Pushkara is mortally afraid of heights? That was the first thing Nala said during the royal feast when the brothers were exchanging banter.'

She scooped water and dripped it playfully on Hemanga's head, 'Let your head cool, golden bird! You have started hallucinating too much.' Hemanga let the water drip not bothering to shake it away. An awkward silence thickened between them and she started humming a song and applying turmeric paste on her body. 'Don't worry, Hemanga. I know how to protect myself. My father has brought me up well. I won't let the lust of someone curtail my freedom and joy. I know how to put him in his place,' she reassured him.

A shadow fell on them and a pair of hands covered Damayanti's eyes from behind, making her gasp. She grabbed the hand and pushed her assailant into the water. Nala broke the surface of the water, sputtering and coughing. 'Now who is surprised?' Damayanti asked. He grabbed her ankle and pulled her into the water. Their peals of laughter echoed in the bathing ghat. They raced to the jasmine island in the middle of the pond and Damayanti beat Nala to it.

'Well, swimming is not what I am famous for,' Nala said playfully.

'Ah, except in your culinary skill, you can never beat me in anything, Nala,' Damayanti splashed water at her husband.

Nala smiled at her and gave a piercing whistle, startling her.

'What?' she asked. The neigh of a horse startled her. She saw the black horse of Nala standing at the shore of the pond. Nala whistled again, this time in a different tone and the horse started prancing around.

'How?' Damayanti was amazed.

'Aswahrudya. I can talk to horses. I know their language,' said Nala.

'Don't bluff,' responded Damayanti in disbelief.

'Watch this,' Nala smiled and began to let out a series of whistles and commands. The horse galloped around the pond, stood on its hind legs, prattled around rhythmically and with the final command, jumped into the pond, drenching them with water.

'I can make him gallop as fast as the wind,' Nala boasted.

'Still, I will beat you,' Damayanti cried. The horse neighed, startling her and throwing her into his arms.

Laughing and playfully hurling water at each other, they were blissful in their world. There was no time for the bird to convince either of them or for them to heed its warning. So Hemanga spread his wings and flew off. The frolicking sounds of the happy couple made the dread he was feeling, heavier. Sick with worry, Hemanga soared higher to the sky and circled the city.

The Nishada city was breathtakingly beautiful to watch from the heights. Forests radiated from all sides. Silver cascades of winding rivers glistened brightly and the occasional orange of the fire of forest trees broke the monotony of green here and there. But Hemanga knew the shadow of Kali lurked somewhere beneath, like a crouching tiger waiting to pounce on the deer herd.

Listless, Hemanga continued to hover above the city for the rest of the day. By evening, he saw Nala and Damayanti ride out of the fort, racing their horses and disappearing into the jungle. They were laughing and teasing each other all the way.

Hemanga was about to follow them when he heard the distant notes of a flute. Soon, the rhythmic clangs of cymbals and rolls of drums intensified.

A group of bards was approaching the city. Shadows of banyan trees had lengthened in the mud path that snaked its way to the fort. He saw the gang bursting out of the jungle into the clearing that lay between the fort gate and the forest. The melody from the flute and the gong of the cymbals became louder. A train of jugglers walked behind the musicians.

Men and women dressed in rainbow-hued clothes and turbans of myriad colours danced behind them. Some walked with performing monkeys on chains. Bear dancers led their dark furry beasts behind them. An elephant that had intricate white designs all over its body ambled by, carrying many dwarfs on its howdah. Two camels treaded lazily, peering at the world with disdain. In the rear of the procession, a yogi with flowing white beard sauntered with an amiable smile.

The procession halted before the fort door. The soldiers watched them with curiosity. Three drummers stepped forward and started beating their drums furiously. A bard started crooning and the dancers rushed forward to perform practised synchronized moves. Soon the clearing before the fort exploded in a blaze of colours and sound. Horses danced along to the rhythm, performing monkeys did somersaults and pranced around on two legs. The painted elephant balanced on one foot on a tripod and then stood on its head. Jugglers juggled first with wooden clubs and then with daggers.

The fort doors creaked open and the performing gangs danced into the city with people cheering for them, from either side of the path. The children danced in front of the procession raising clouds of dust. The drummers of the Nishada city came out with their wares too. The Nishada drums answered with rigour, prompting the men who were drinking toddy in the tavern to rush out and break into an impromptu dance. To the clap and cheer of the people, the guests and the hosts competed.

Hemanga was perched on the half-built temple tower watching the mendicant who sat cross-legged under the banyan tree before the temple. There was something suspicious about the man. The sanyasi's eyes wandered around in the crowd. From the dusty clouds that the dancing feet had thickened, a man stepped forward. His face was covered with the tail of his turban. Hemanga knew who the newcomer was.

'Ha! Prince Pushkara,' the sanyasi smiled; and the prince shushed him, 'Don't take my name.'

The mendicant smiled.

Pushkara said, 'I . . . I never thought you would come.'

'I came in your dream as commanded by him. I came in person as ordered by him,' the sanyasi responded, his eyes glittering.

Pushkara looked scared. He leaned towards the sanyasi and asked, 'Have . . . have you come ready, Swami Dvapara?'

In reply, the holy man raised his right palm and grabbed something from thin air. 'Tell me a number,' he said. Pushkara blinked, staring at the tightly held fist of the holy man. So he repeated again, 'Hmm, tell me a number.'

'One thousand,' Pushkara said.

'Fool, tell me a number from the game of dice.'

'Eight.'

'Eight?' Swami Dvapara smiled and started shaking the dice in his palm.

'By the grace of Kali, the God of fortune and misfortune, give me eight,' Dvapara chanted and rolled the pair of dice on the floor. It spun around and rested at six. Pushkara frowned and at the next moment as if nudged by an invisible hand, one of the dice rolled again. 'Eight!' Swami Dvapara chuckled triumphantly.

Pushkara extended his hands to pick up the dice.

Swami Dvapara snatched it away, 'Not so easy, not so quick.' Then he whispered something in Pushkara's ear, and the prince nodded. Hemanga saw the prince vanishing into the crowd. A moment later his shadow followed him. Dvapara looked at the shadow and bowed deeply. Then the mendicant spread a black silk sheet. He arranged the game of dyuta, the cross-shaped cloth board with neatly divided boxes and sixteen coins made of beads and ivory, by its side. He clapped and beckoned, 'Come on, everyone. Here is your chance to be rich. By the grace of Kali.'

* * *

The gambling began in earnest. Many Nishadas bet against Dvapara and lost. By sunset, most of the cattle, sheep, and goats of the Nishadas had become the property of Swami Dvapara. As the night hulked and greyed, the gambling continued in the light of a torch. The singers and acrobats had transformed into warriors and they guarded the winnings they had robbed from the Nishadas by standing in a circle around them. By midnight, the Nishadas had lost everything. They stood forlorn and angry. A riot was on near simmer when Pushkara arrived on his horse.

'What is happening here?' he asked, feigning surprise. The women quickly crowded around his horse, beseeching him to save their husbands from ruin. He became indignant at the men's folly.

'The dice are loaded. There is some black magic in them,' the men cried in their defence. 'They have cheated us. We should slay them all.'

'Tear them from limb to limb. Stone them!' Angry voices shook the whole city.

* * *

Hemanga knew the situation had gone out of control and that he ought to find Nala right away. He flew into the night, suppressing his fear of darkness, with the apprehension of getting tricked by Kali in an attempt to stop him. Beyond the insipid light of the city, the jungle was dark and mysterious and scared Hemanga to death. Yet he knew he had to find Nala before a battle broke out between the Nishadas and Swami Dvapara's men.

'Nala . . . Damayanti . . .' his cry pierced the wilderness, echoing down the hills and valleys below. From somewhere, a tiger roared. A pale moon clung to a purple sky. Hemanga could feel someone following him. He hurled through the thick foliage, flying blind and crying in panic. Finally, he found Nala and Damayanti sleeping in each other's arms by a brook. Their horses stood a few feet away munching fresh grass.

'Your country is ruined, and you are sleeping here,' he screamed. Nala woke up, startled by the sudden cry. Hemanga tried to explain the grave situation in the fort but in his panic, he was incoherent at best. He spoke in swan tongue and Damayanti awoke with a yawn.

When she saw Hemanga and heard his babble, she chuckled. 'He is in panic and is blabbering,' Nala said. Damayanti held Hemanga's head between her palms and talked soothingly to him. Calmed by her gentle voice and the caresses, Hemanga broke down and told them all that he had witnessed and about the serious danger the Nishada country faced. The beautiful couple's faces turned pallid. Soon they were galloping through the jungle to the fort, with Hemanga perched on Damayanti's shoulder.

11

Game of Dyuta

The eastern sky was bleeding red when they entered the fort. They could hear the clash of swords, angry yells, and blood-curdling screams. They dashed through the main avenue and Nala yelled at the fighting mob, 'Stop! Stop! Your king commands you to stop fighting.'

The two warring sides parted for the horses to pass. Dead men with severed limbs, headless torsos and corpses with their gut wrenched out lay all around the temple courtyard. They saw Pushkara covered in blood and grime. He had his sword raised high in his right hand and with the left, he had gripped Swami Dvapara by his long hair.

'Stop, stop!' Nala yelled as he jumped off his saddle and ran to his brother.

He gripped Pushkara's wrist but the prince struggled to free himself, saying 'Leave me, brother, this scoundrel must die.'

Swami Dvapara did not exhibit any fear. He stared at Pushkara and said plainly, 'Go ahead, cut off my head.'

'What is happening here?' Nala asked.

'Your Highness,' Dvapara addressed Nala, 'I did not rob them at knifepoint. They volunteered to play dice with me. And lost.'

'He's a cheat, his dice is enchanted,' Pushkara cried and slammed Dvapara against the tree.

'You are a nobleman, your highness,' Swami Dvapara said. 'Do you think killing me is fair?'

'My people have become poor; they have lost everything by their folly. I beg you to be kind and return some of their wealth,' Nala said with folded hands.

Swami Dvapara smiled, 'I have no need for the wealth of others. It was just a game.' A wave of relief washed over the crowd. The Swami paused and then said, 'However, as per the rules of dyuta, the winner never parts with his winnings unless he is defeated in the game.'

'But you just said . . . ' Nala said slowly.

Hemanga could not refrain himself anymore, so he cried aloud, 'Beware Nala, beware!' But Nala raised his hand to silence the bird and addressed Swami Dvapara.

'How can I get back my people's money?' Nala asked Dvapara.

Swami Dvapara ran his fingers through his long beard and said, 'There are two ways. One, you can take back everything by force. You can kill us all.'

'And the second way?' Nala asked, his eyes hardening.

'Win.' There was silence. Swami Dvapara added, 'Win, against me in the game of dice.'

The deadly silence stretched as Nala stood brooding. Damayanti moved towards her husband and said, 'Take the first option Nala, don't even think about the second.'

Dvapara chuckled, 'Of course, the first option is what a Nishada would take. A Nishada need not worry about the code of noble kshatriyas. Kill us all and take back everything.' Hemanga knew the game Kali was playing. He was stoking the deepest fear in Nala's mind: the need to be recognized as a great king and not an upstart Nishada.

Hemanga cried out, 'Please don't do this Nala! This is a bait. The dice is loaded with the evil of Kali.' But in that charged moment not a man or beast paid attention to the bird. Damayanti stood leaning on the Peepal tree, her face tense, fists clenched. Hemanga fluttered to her. 'Please stop him,' Hemanga pleaded but she stood in a daze.

Wordlessly the two men came to a pact. Hemanga watched Damayanti's eyes glisten with unshed tears as they settled down to play. A thousand pair of eyes watched as the dice started to roll. Nala won the first round and the crowd cheered as a pair of bullocks was restored to its owner. The dice rolled again and again, and Nala continued with his winning streak.

Dvapara said smoothly, 'See, luck is favouring you, my king, or are you an expert player?'

Nala smiled nervously, 'I have never played the game of dyuta in my life. I detest gambling.'

'Oh, you should play more, my king. It is the game of Gods,' Dvapara said quietly, his eyes fixed on the game.

Hemanga muttered angrily, 'The game of your God indeed, the game of Kali!'

Nala continued to win and it was nearly dawn when the last of the cattle were recovered. Nala said, 'That is it.'

Damayanti heaved a sigh of relief. Dvapara sat smiling. Nala was about to get up when a young mother rushed from the crowd and fell on the king's feet, 'Swami! My daughter, my daughter!' She was sobbing incessantly. Nala lifted her up and she said, 'My daughter, she is barely three years old and . . . ' The woman broke down.

Dvapara said smoothly, 'Her husband staked his three-year-old daughter and lost.'

'Who gambled his daughter,' Nala trembled with rage. The crowd pushed and shoved a derelict Nishada. He reeked of toddy and decay. With a stupid grin that showed his betel-stained teeth, the Nishada hiccupped as he bowed and said, 'I had to settle my debts at the tavern, and I needed money, Your Highness.'

'The drunkard sold my daughter, swami,' the woman cried. 'Help me!'

Nala turned to Dvapara, 'You accepted a little girl as a stake?'

'Kings even gamble with their kingdoms your Highness. What is a three-year-old urchin? If your subject is desperate enough to stake his daughter, ask yourself whether you are a good enough king?'

Nala stood silent while the mother wailed and beat her chest. She repeatedly touched Nala's feet and pleaded with him to reclaim her daughter.

The drunkard husband yelled at her, 'Stop troubling the king, woman. You are wailing as if I pawned our son. It is just the girl.'

Nala couldn't stand it anymore. He once again sat down cross-legged before Dvapara. Hemanga's heart sank. The swan knew this was the beginning of the end. The dice started rolling, twisting the destiny of Nala in its wake. Hemanga could hear the laughter of Kali in the air. One by one the king started losing everything. Nala didn't put any of his subject's possession at stake. First, he put his horses, then his treasures in the palace, then the palace followed, and finally the throne itself. Damayanti watched with growing indignation and despair as her husband lost everything before her eyes.

His subjects stood shocked at the turn of events. Yet no one staked their things for the sake of the man who had won back all they had lost some time ago. A few women wept, for tears are cheap. Many whispered that Nala was paying the price for his arrogance.

'I have nothing more to offer,' Nala said, his head bent in shame. The little girl for whom he had staked his kingdom was yet to be won back.

'Yes, you have,' the mendicant smiled and eyed Damayanti from head to toe. Damayanti shuddered at the suggestion. 'Nala,' her voice trembled. Nala drew his sword in anger and pointed it at Dvapara.

Dvapara chuckled, 'Thank you. That sword is now mine,' He took it from Nala's hand and kept it aside. Nala stared at the sword that had been his faithful servant since his childhood.

Dvapara asked, 'Are you staking your only possession for one last try? If you win, you win it all, if you lose you only lose her. You can always have another wife,' Dvapara suggested helpfully.

'No, she is not my possession to stake, she is my *ardhangini*, the half of my body, the whole of my soul,' Nala said softly. Hemanga wept. He had known it would end up like this only.

Damayanti looked at her husband with tear-filled eyes, 'Stake me Nala. I wish to share your fate, if you are a slave, I am one too.'

Nala shook his head, 'My fate is my own. I didn't marry you only to give you away to a gambler. You are free to go, marry anyone you wish, marry one of the Gods who had come to your swayamvara or marry any noble king. I am a low-caste Nishada with nothing to call as my own. Leave me to my fate.'

And before Damayanti could protest or say anything, Nala turned to Dvapara and said, 'I stake myself.'

The dice rolled again, and all the Nishadas who watched drew their breath as one. Kali won. Nala was now a slave of Swami Dvapara. Damayanti stepped forward and said, 'I stake myself. If I win, free my husband.'

Dvapara smiled, 'No need, Devi. You are already my slave. You are the property of your husband, whether he agrees to it or not, so you cannot stake yourself. You can do nothing that your husband does not permit. And he cannot permit you anything without my consent.'

Damayanti's eyes flashed. 'No. I am not his property. I am his wife, and he didn't stake me when he lost. Now I am staking myself to free him.'

Dvapara laughed, 'Then are you agreeing he is nothing to you?' A murmur rose from the crowd.

'He is my husband!' Damayanti cried.

'If so, then already, you are my slave,' Dvapara chuckled.

'This is ridiculous,' Damayanti retorted.

'Ridicule is what your husband would earn if he doesn't keep his word. He has already become my slave and thus you too have become mine.'

Nala interfered, 'She is free to go. I have already forsaken her before I staked myself, you can't make her your slave.'

Dvapara laughed, 'Brilliant, your husband has forsaken you. Have you forsaken him too?'

Damayanti did not have an answer. Hemanga whispered, 'I had warned you about Kali, you never listened to me.'

'I stake myself,' Pushkara stepped forward.

Damayanti heaved a sigh of relief. 'I wish he wins,' she said.

'Wish he loses, Devi,' Hemanga said, his voice breaking.

Nala embraced his brother. Pushkara took his place before the dyuta board and started rolling the dice. As Hemanga had foreseen, Pushkara started winning. First, he won the horses, then the elephants and chariots. By the eighth game, he had won the kingdom back and all the personal possessions of Nala. Finally, he won the little girl and handed her to the grateful mother. The crowd cheered with each win and hailed Pushkara. Then Pushkara won Nala back.

Dvapara bowed to Pushkara, 'You are a fortunate man, King of Nishadas, you have won.'

Nala turned to Damayanti to embrace her, 'My brother has won, we have won back everything.' Damayanti stood stiff not embracing her husband back, her eyes never leaving her brother-in-law. 'Pushkara, King of Nishadas,' she whispered, staring at her brother-in-law.

'You have won,' Dvapara said to Pushkara, 'the most beautiful of all women, Damayanti.'

Pushkara looked over his shoulders and smiled at Damayanti, 'Yes I have.'

Nala heard it and laughed, 'Yes, brother, you have freed me and your sister-in-law.'

Pushkara ignored Nala and moved towards Damayanti, 'I have won you and you belong to me now. I am the King of Nishadas, and you are my queen.'

The crowd watched with bated breath. There were surprised murmurs, but no one spoke a word against their new king. Nala was too shocked to react.

Dvapara said, 'He has spoken wisely, Nishadas. He won the kingdom that his foolish brother gambled and lost.'

Someone in the crowd roared, 'Jai Maharaja Pushkara, Jai Maharani Damayanti.'

Nala staggered back, 'Stop! Stop your pranks, brother,' he laughed nervously, 'she's your sister-in-law, the one to be respected like your mother.'

Dvapara sneered, 'Get lost, you slave.' Damayanti glowered at her brother-in-law. She stood unflinching. 'You are my slave now, but you can be my queen,' Pushkara said with a crooked smile.

Damayanti ignored him and turned to Dvapara, 'You are a learned brahmin. Does the master have the right over the slave's wife? Remember, I was never staked.'

'Your husband is my slave and so are you. I can do whatever I please with you,' Pushkara's eyes flared up in anger.

Damayanti ignored him and waited for Dvapara to answer. Hemanga knew what the answer would be. Dvapara shook his dice in the cup of his palms, closed his eyes, and said, 'It is a difficult question to answer, the Dharmashastras are silent on it.'

'To hell with your Dharmashastras,' Pushkara cried impatiently, 'Damayanti is mine!' Dvapara raised his palm to demand silence and rattled the dice together. 'Let the dice decide her fate. Let God Kali say what is right.'

Hemanga knew what Kali, the God of misfortune and luck, would decide even before the dice had stopped rolling. Separating Damayanti from Nala by force would prove nothing for Kali. For him, only Damayanti voluntarily giving up Nala would prove his point.

The dice came to a standstill and Dvapara exclaimed, 'Aah, it says you have no right on her unless her husband gives her to you. Nala could be your slave, but you have no right on Damayanti since she was never staked.'

Pushkara slammed his fist on the tree, roaring, 'This is unfair! You cheat, you promised . . . I brought you here!'

Dvapara was his serene self. Suddenly Pushkara came to his senses. In his rage he had exposed his conspiracy. His gaze met that of Damayanti, and he looked away.

Nala, with tear-filled eyes, whispered, 'I brought you up like a son. You weren't just a younger brother, Pushkara.'

Hemanga cried, 'Nishadas, can't you see it. This viper Pushkara conspired with that charlatan Dvapara. He is possessed by the evil Kali. Please arise against Pushkara and depose him. Nala is your king.'

The Nishadas, however, stood shuffling their feet and looking down. Pushkara snapped, 'I don't care for any Dharmashastras. Damayanti is mine.'

'Then my husband will fight you as per the ancient code of Nishadas,' Damayanti said, coldly.

'Son, a good player must know when to stop,' Dvapara said with a grin. Pushkara stood indecisive while the clamour grew among the mob. Hemanga wished Pushkara would accept the challenge of Damayanti and choose to fight Nala.

'Get out of my country,' Pushkara snarled. 'Begone with your wife and never come back. The kingdom is mine now.'

Nala was about to argue when Damayanti held his wrist, 'Let us go away from this accursed land.'

She started walking, holding Nala's hand. Defeat did not weigh her down. She walked erect and proud like a conquering monarch while Nala walked as if he was carrying a mountain of shame on his shoulders. The crowd parted, making way for them. Hemanga, angry and desperate, turned to hurl abuses at Pushkara when the new king clapped his hands and hailed the departing figures. Damayanti stopped in her tracks, her fiery eyes burning like an ember; but Nala walked towards his brother, hope glimmering in his eyes.

'Where are you going with my things?' snarled Pushkara. 'I own everything you wear, including your clothes.' The crowd gasped. 'Strip him naked,' Pushkara ordered his soldiers.

Damayanti tore off her *uthariya*, the upper cloth, into two and handed half to her husband. 'We don't want anything that belongs to this demon,' she said. Pushkara yanked away Nala's loin waistcloth and Damayanti covered her husband's nakedness with the strip of cloth. Some men in the crowd laughed at the fall of the man who had ruled them as a king for nearly a decade. A few wept at his misfortune.

Holding Nala's hand, Damayanti walked out of the Nishada city. Behind her, the sky lowered the sun into its nightly grave.

12

Nala's Fear

They had been walking the whole night and the better part of the next day and were tired of hunger, sadness, and thirst. Nala had not spoken a word since they had left the Nishada kingdom. Damayanti had given up attempting to talk to him. When Nala saw the temple, he limped towards it and collapsed on its steps. He sat on the dusty floor and leaned on a pillar, staring ahead with a vacant expression.

'Nala,' Damayanti called him softly. 'Let us not despair. If we don't give up hope, nothing is lost.'

Nala said, 'You . . . you should go to your father's home.'

Damayanti's eyes flashed in anger. 'Enough of this whining. Wherever my husband is, that is my home.'

'I don't have a home now, Damayanti, I am destitute.'

Damayanti snapped, 'I didn't marry you because you are the King of the Nishadas. I married you because I love you. I had enough kings and emperors seeking my hand. I even had the Gods seeking my hand, remember?'

'I am a Nishada and I had forgotten my place for some time. Now, the Gods have shown me my place. This is my destiny.'

'You have not just lost the kingdom, you have lost your wits too, Nala. You are talking like a fool.'

'You said it right, I am a fool. I dragged you into the cesspool of my misfortune,' Nala's voice cracked.

Damayanti sprang up and stood before Nala, 'You are not the first king to lose your kingdom, nor would you be the last. Enough of this talk.' Tears sparkled in her eyes. Nala covered his face and his shoulders heaved. Damayanti's voice softened. She sat by his side and pulled him towards her bosom. He wrapped his hands around her and wept. Hemanga watched them, feeling angry at Nala and admiration for Damayanti.

'Nala, please, nothing is lost yet. Let us fight back and win our kingdom.'

'We can't fight.'

'Why not?' Damayanti's voice had an edge now.

'Because what is lost in a game of dice can only be won through a game of dice.'

'Who said so?' Damayanti asked.

'That is the dharma. I cannot use violence.'

Damayanti had reached the end of her patience. 'Let us talk about this some other day. Now I am hungry, find me some food.'

Nala stood up wearily and said, 'I don't know where I will find food in this jungle.'

'You don't know? Make a bow and some arrows and hunt. You are a Nishada.' Nala stood without moving, staring at his feet.

Damayanti asked carefully, 'Now what, Nala?'

'Hunt,' Nala whispered, 'a Nishada should hunt. You said it right.'

'Oh, God! I didn't mean it like that,' Damayanti cried. Nala started walking, looking straight ahead.

Damayanti ran behind him, 'I don't want you to go now. Please stay here, I will find food.' She faked a smile, 'I'm not even hungry.'

Nala said, 'I had vowed not to kill any being. I had embraced ahimsa. But you are right. A Nishada has no right to take such noble vows. You are right.'

Hemanga could not stand it anymore. He yelled, 'Find some fruits, find some wild berries, mangoes or yam, if you don't want to hunt.'

Nala stood as if stung. Then without looking at Hemanga, he walked listlessly into the jungle.

'Devi, stop him. Let him not go now,' Hemanga pleaded to Damayanti.

'Leave him alone for some time, Hemanga. He is shaken but he will come around. Let him find some food for us all. Not that I can't hunt or lay a snare or gather some berries but if I do that, it will shatter his esteem. A man should feel his wife is dependent on him and not the other way round.'

'Big words, lady, big words,' Hemanga cried, 'but are you not seeing it?'

'What?'

'Look, open your eyes and see!'

Damayanti stared at the vanishing figure of Nala. The jungle was swallowing his forlorn form. 'What?' Damayanti asked.

Hemanga cried, 'Can't you see it? Behind him, look.'

'Behind him? I see nothing except his shadow.'

Hemanga exclaimed, looking at the leering figure of Kali crawling behind Nala, 'Can't you see it, Devi? The shadow behind the shadow?'

'What?'

'Kali has got hold of Nala. He has possessed him now. Nala is not himself anymore.'

'I know,' Damayanti said. 'We have had tough luck.'

'You don't understand,' Hemanga tapped his feet impatiently. 'It is no ordinary ill-luck. Kali is determined to ruin Nala and you. It was Kali who possessed the dice and turned and twisted it against Nala.'

'Enough,' Damayanti said. 'No power in the universe can part us. Nothing can blacken Nala's heart. He can never be evil.'

Hemanga wanted to say, to be evil, one need not be bad at heart. One can do the noblest of things and evil can spring spontaneously out of it. One can do the best of things and be punished for it. The ways of Kali were incomprehensible but Hemanga knew that saying such things would only make Damayanti lose hope, and he knew that wouldn't be good. Hope is the flickering torch that would show her the path in the darkness that was enveloping her life. Without a word, Hemanga took off. He wanted to keep an eye on Nala. After flying for some time, he realized that Nala was nowhere to be seen. It was as if the jungle had swallowed the banished Nishada king.

The mist sneaking from the bushes dragged the cloak of night in its wake.

13

Despair

Shadows crowded around Nala as he stumbled forward blindly. Creepers extended their fronds to grab him. It grew darker and the night caved in on him. Nothing made sense. One moment he was the king of a prosperous land, frolicking in the arms of the most beautiful woman on earth and in another moment, he had been stripped of everything: his home, his land, his clothes. His own blood, his brother had shattered him completely. He heard howls and screams. He heard laughter echoing around. He heard garbled voices mocking his plight, his rags, the darkness of his skin, his caste, everything. He was going insane.

'You worthless low-life. You wanted to marry a high-born. Shame on you,' the voices yelled. Nala punched the air, bared his teeth, and challenged the invisibles to come forth and fight. 'Damayanti is mine. Mine!' He shouted hoarse and the voice cackled in laughter from the bushes.

Nala wanted to tear out the hair from his scalp. He wept silently, covering his face with both hands, his shoulders shaking with grief. Life was so fragile, so transient. In just one flick of fate's wrist, a kingdom was snatched from him. Here he was stumbling in a forest, dethroned, humiliated by a mere game. The ruler of a land where his gestures and words were law, was now just a mendicant. Shadows shifted, trees murmured and from beyond the hills, hyenas howled. Wind rustled through the bamboo grooves and whispered in his ears, 'Fool, did you catch anything?'

Nala yelled, 'No, I can't hunt.' And a voice whispered in his ears, 'You are worthless. Do you know why?' A pregnant silence reigned, and then in his other ear a voice said in a hushed tone, 'because you are a low-life Nishada.'

Nala retorted in a feverish voice, 'I can't let her go hungry. I will kill for her. I can't let her go hungry.' In answer, he heard an owl hoot.

'Mocking me? Mocking me?' Nala yelled at the owl perched on the high branch of a kadamba tree. He removed his loincloth, his last possession in the world, and twisted it to make a lasso.

He flung the lasso at the bird and it caught the owl by its feet. It flew away carrying his last possession with it. Nala stood stunned, not knowing what to do. Starkly conscious of his nakedness, he let out a cry of anguish and started staggering through the jungle like a maniac.

* * *

Meanwhile, in the dilapidated temple, Damayanti was getting worried. *Where had Nala gone?* There was no trace of Hemanga too. Except for the occasional wind that rustled the dry leaves and sped past her, an uneasy silence reigned. A dull moon rose in the sky. Sounds of scurrying animals came from the bushes. The thickets seemed to have grown bigger in the deepening darkness. As the night became colder and mist enveloped the temple, she became frantic with worry.

Sitting there, idly waiting for Nala to appear was futile. She must do something to assuage the guilt that was overwhelming her. She shouldn't have sent him alone, she thought. What if evil thoughts had possessed him, what if in the grip of despair, he decided to end it all? She hurried into the forest calling her beloved's name. 'Nala, Nala!' Her forlorn cries were swallowed by the silence of the jungle. She did not see the pair of eyes staring at her as she stumbled past a banyan tree.

A man stepped out of the hiding and watched her hurrying across the meadow. He gave a low whistle and a dog crashed out of the bushes. The man notched his bow on his shoulders and re-tied the quiver of arrows to his waist. He started following Damayanti and the dog trotted behind him.

14

The Curse

The sky had started to lighten up in the east when Nala reached by the shore of a mountain stream. His throat was parched with thirst. The gurgle of the brook was heavenly to his ears. He crawled on all fours to drink water from the stream like a thirsty beast. Nala had hardly taken a gulp of the cool water when he was startled by a hiss behind his ears.

For a moment, his body froze in fear. A huge king cobra was struggling to get out of a thorny bush that lay half-bent into the water. Then, in the next moment, his inborn chivalry kicked in. 'Poor fellow you are going to hurt yourself. Let me save you,' Nala said as he waddled towards the trapped snake. The cobra spread its hood menacingly. This time Nala said in a soothing voice, 'I have come to help you, I am not your enemy.' The cobra shrunk its hood and lay limp. Nala carefully removed the sharp thorns from the snake's scales and took it out from the thorn bush.

'Now go back to your family,' Nala said smilingly and the cobra struck at his feet. Before he could even scream, Nala collapsed on the grass unconscious. The snake slithered over his body and vanished into the jungle. The shadow of Kali hovered

over the inert figure of Nala for some time. Then it solidified
into the form of a bat and flew away.

* * *

Damayanti reached the mountain stream, where it took a steep
plunge into the valley. In the orange glow of the dawn, the
place was mesmerizing, but she was in no state of mind to
appreciate the beauty. The thunderous roar of the waterfall
filled her with dread instead. She saw a rag fluttering in wind,
trapped on a fern at the edge of the cliff and a shudder passed
through her spine. It was the piece of her uthariya she had
given to Nala. She inched towards the precipice where the
stream took a graceful leap.

Damayanti had expected Nala to be lying dead at the foot
of the waterfall. The rock was slippery with moss so she had
to crawl on her belly to safely reach the edge of the cliff. She
desperately tried to keep her foothold on the sparse fern that
grew in its crevice because a slip would have been fatal. Just then,
an owl fluttered past with a hoot, startling her. A crab scurried
away for cover. The spray from the cascade had drenched her as
she crawled froward. She was precariously close to the edge of
the rock. Damayanti craned her neck and peeped down. Water
plunged down in sheets and splattered into a million droplets. A
rainbow softly arched across the view. There was no inert body
of Nala at the bottom as she had feared.

On either bank, the bushes swayed merrily in the breeze.
Butterflies and dragonflies flitted about in a graceful dance.
Nature was serene and indifferent. Damayanti heaved a sigh
of relief and was about to turn back when she felt something
grip her ankle. Something powerful. When she looked, it was
a python. It was wrapping itself around her limbs. She yelled

in panic and pulled her leg away, losing her footing. The next instant she was plunging headlong into the ravine. Damayanti could see the rock at the bottom of the falls approaching her at breakneck speed and cringed her eyes shut. When she came back to her senses, she realized that she had not in fact fallen into the waterfall but was dangling mid-air. She hadn't pulled free from the python completely—or it must have lunged back at her as she fell. Whatever it was, the python was now coiled around her waist—her only link to the terrain above—and was inching closer towards her face. She was hanging upside down in the grip of the python. The roar of the waterfall muted her desperate cries for help.

* * *

Nala woke up feeling exhausted. He faintly remembered that he had met with an accident. The thorn bush looked forlorn and empty. He sat up rubbing his groggy eyes and stopped suddenly. He stared at his palm. There was something wrong. His long shapely fingers had shrunk into pudgy, little, knobby ones. A cold dread started solidifying in his veins. Trembling, he raised his left arm and to his shock, that appeared misshapen too. Then he looked at his legs and jumped in fright. His feet had shrunk, legs contracted. He gasped as he felt his nose, which was stubbed flat. Even his lips had thickened like berries.

He stood up and the ground appeared nearer than he had ever remembered. He ran to the stream. He instinctively knew that something was terribly wrong. When he saw his reflection in a puddle near the stream, he let out a shriek of agony. He frantically touched his face, shoulders, knees, and nose. He stared at his reflection and once again let out a deep cry. A dwarf was staring back at him. He was barely three feet in height. The reflection had a scant resemblance with the handsome face that Nala was used to seeing in his mirrors.

A sinister laughter boomed in the air, 'You dirty Nishada! Now I have taken away the last of your good fortune. A couple of days ago you were the hero of the Nishadas. You were the most handsome of all men on earth. A king with a beautiful bride to love, you challenged the Gods to marry Damayanti. Now you have become what you deserved to be—an ugly dwarf with not even a leaf to cover your nakedness.'

The laughter echoed around. In a fit of desperation, Nala jumped into the stream to end it all, but as if kicked by someone, he bounced back. He lay panting on the grass for some time. The thoughts of Damayanti seeing him now haunted him and he once again ran to the stream to end his life. He was flung back to the shore again by an invisible force.

'Nishada, if you die, Damayanti would be just a grieving widow. That is not what I want. I want her to forsake you. I want her to say, she can't live with an ugly dwarf who does not own even a loincloth to cover his shame. Live and suffer, Nishada. That is Kali's blessing for you.'

A bat then burst out of the bush on his left and flew away into the beyond. The shriek of its laughter hung heavy in the air for some more time. Nala lay on the grass stunned at the turn of his fate, wondering what wrong he had done to be haunted by fate like this. He was startled by the flap of wings. He saw Hemanga, but crawled to hide behind the bush and waited until the forlorn bird went away, calling out his name.

Nala plucked a few dry leaves from the ground and fashioned a loincloth with a vine by stringing them together. He waddled across the stream not even bothering about the slippery rocks and the swift currents for he knew he was immortal in his misfortune. He should keep away from Damayanti, he decided, so that Kali would stop troubling her. He crossed the river and continued north. 'Wherever you are, my beloved, be happy and forget this unfortunate low caste,' Nala whispered as he walked, as if talking to Damayanti. The jungle around him continued in its rhythm, indifferent to the plight of anyone.

In the theatre of life, there were endless plays. What was the fortune or the misfortune of a puny man in the grand order of its things? The day would give way to night, and sun to the moon and stars. Leaves would fall and sprout again. The breeze would blow through the trees, clouds would sail through the skies, and the tide would come and go. Rain and mist, drought and flood, spring and autumn, winter and summer—all would appear and return backstage, again and again. Life would follow death and death would shadow life. Why care for a man—giant or dwarf, noble or evil, high or low?

The concert of life goes on and on.

15

The Hunter

The man who had been following Damayanti saw the accident that befell her and ran towards the cliff. His dog yelped and ran behind. He was a hunter and was smitten by the lovely woman wandering in the forest. She appeared high-born and he was scared to approach her, but now fate had opened a path to him. The hunter saw how the python had wound half its body on a tree stump in the rock and the half around Damayanti's waist. The hunter knew he had to be careful. If he startled the snake, it would drop its prey and the beautiful woman would fall to her death.

'Amavasi, quiet,' he hushed his dog. It crouched at the edge of the cliff, wagging its tale. The hunter gently pulled the python up. When he got hold of Damayanti's ankle, the hunter took out a knife from his waistband and cleaved the python in two halves in one swift slash. One half of the python uncoiled from Damayanti's waist and spiralled into the bottom of the fall. The other half lashed around on the rock splattering blood all around. The dog barked and danced around the dying snake and licked the blood.

Damayanti, half-unconscious in her fright, opened her eyes and realized she was not dead yet. A dusty unwashed face grinned at her. She was still dangling upside down from the cliff.

'Save me,' Damayanti cried.

'Woman, you are so beautiful,' the hunter leered.

A bat came from somewhere and fluttered around her face. Damayanti screamed in fear, 'Please don't leave me! Lift me up please!'

'I always wanted a beautiful wife, but no woman ever wanted me,' the hunter said and gently swayed her from side to side. Earth spun around her.

'What do you say?' the hunter asked Damayanti.

'Help me,' she cried desperately.

'I will help you if you promise you will be mine.'

'I will always be grateful to you,' said Damayanti. The world was swimming around her eyes and the bat gave a shriek of laughter. I'm hallucinating, Damayanti thought.

'Do you promise to marry me, be my woman?' the hunter asked.

Damayanti could barely hear his voice over the thundering roar of the waterfall. 'I will do anything. Please don't drop me,' she cried.

Slowly the hunter lifted her up from the abyss and placed her on the rock. She slowly opened her eyes to stare at the lean face of the mongrel. The dog gave a short yelp as if welcoming her back to life.

'Amavasi, stay back and allow the lady to breathe,' the hunter said, and the dog backtracked. Damayanti sat up breathing heavily, her body was still trembling. The hunter squatted near her and bared his lips into a lopsided grin that showed his stained teeth. 'I saved your life,' he said.

'Thank you,' Damayanti smiled at him tiredly.

'Let us go to our village,' he said, grabbing her wrist.

She yanked her hand back, 'I am in search of my husband.'

'Husband?' the hunter laughed. 'You have found him? I am your husband now.' The hunter laughed again.

'I am the wife of Nala, the King of Nishadas.'

'Ho! Our queen,' the hunter stood up, eyeing her suspiciously. 'Why should our queen roam around in this jungle with not even a servant to accompany her? You look dirt poor.' He snickered, adding, 'If you are a queen, then I am Lord Indra, the King of Devas, and this Amavasi is not a dog but Airavatha, the white elephant of Indra.' Then guffawing at his own joke, the hunter grabbed her hand again.

'Don't dare to touch me,' she snapped.

'Aha! Aha, what a grateful woman. I saved you.'

'Thank you for your . . .'

'To hell with your thanks,' the hunter said, grabbing her wrists. 'Keep your word, woman. I will take you to my village. We will have a proper wedding ceremony. There will be roasted deer meat and gooseberry brew for the feast. I will get a boar stewed for you.' Damayanti did not know what possessed her but her skills from years of martial arts training as the Princess of Vidarbha kicked in. She stomped her right foot forward, gripped the hunter by his armpit, and flipped him above her head.

A scream brought her back to senses. She saw him toppling down the cliff, and a moment later, came the sickening thud, followed by a splash. The river swallowed the hunter and carried him away in its frothing arms. Damayanti stood at the cliff edge, looking down, feeling nothing. The dog's reaction brought her back to her senses. The poor creature made a leap to follow its master but Damayanti caught it. It bit her hand, but she held it firm, 'No, no, my dear.' The dog struggled to be free, to die with its master. The shock hit her and she broke down.

'You ungrateful wretch,' a voice boomed around her. 'You killed the one who helped you.' Damayanti, shattered by her grief, pressed her face to the chest of the dog, and cried, 'I know, but I had no choice, he tried to force himself on me.'

The dog stared at the abyss where its master had vanished and whimpered. The hunter may have only given a morsel of leftover to the creature, yet it wanted to die for him. And she had killed the man who saved her life.

'Nala is suffering for your sin,' from nowhere came Kali's voice. 'Forsake him and he shall cease to suffer.'

'Yes, I sinned by killing my saviour, but I did it to save my honour,' she yelled back. 'I will carry the guilt forever, but that is not going to stop me from loving Nala.'

Kali's laughter filled the air, 'Then go and find him and see what your sin has done to your handsome husband.'

The speck of shadow burst into a loud boom and an uneasy silence descended. Damayanti stood up with determination and said to the dog, 'Come with me, dear.' Amavasi hesitated, weighing its earlier decision to follow its master to his death or live. His lust for life won and the dog started trotting behind Damayanti at a safe distance.

Though she had put up a brave face to Kali, she knew she would never forget the guilt of killing the hunter. Damayanti moved forward. For now, her only mission was to find her Nala.

16

The Dwarf

The dog ran to a bush and started barking at it. Damayanti stopped. For a moment, her heart skipped a beat. Was Nala somewhere nearby? Her mind was playing games with her. She had been seeing him everywhere. When the wind rustled the bamboo groves, she thought it was his footsteps. When a shadow moved in the woods, her heart leaped in hope. It had been like this. All along, Amavasi followed quietly. It was only when they were halfway past a river bank that Amavasi became excited. Damayanti took a tentative step towards the bush when she heard a flutter of wings above her head. Hemanga landed before her and the dog leaped forward, giving an ear-splitting bark.

'Hey, hey! Easy doggy, easy, easy,' Hemanga cried, fending the dog away by slapping his wings together. Damayanti patted the dog and calmed him. Amavasi sat on its haunches and growled at Hemanga.

'I am sorry, Devi,' Hemanga's voice cracked as he swallowed a sob. 'I lost him.'

'What do you mean?' Damayanti turned pale.

'No, no. Nothing as you fear. He is alive, he is alive.'

'Did you see him?'

'Well err . . . no . . . but he should be alive. He should be searching for you now. But I don't know where he is.'

Damayanti sighed. Amavasi started sniffing the ground and its ears perked in attention. The dog gave a low growl and moved cautiously towards the bush.

'Stop,' Damayanti snapped, and the dog gave a whine and stepped back. 'Nala has abandoned me,' Damayanti said.

'We can't blame him,' Hemanga said cautiously.

'Coward,' Damayanti hissed

'Nala thinks if you are with him, Kali would torment you too. You should marry someone else and . . .'

'Only death can part us. He cannot hide forever. Find him! Tell him he and I, we will face Kali together.'

With an explosive bark, Amavasi leaped at the bush. A panicked cry for help arose and the dog dragged something hideous from the bush. A figure was rolling on the floor and the dog was attacking it furiously. Damayanti pulled the dog back and saw a dwarf covered in blood lying on the grass. Damayanti rushed to him. The dwarf slowly sat up and looked at Damayanti. She shuddered and turned away. Nala lowered his head. He saw the look on her face when she caught sight of his present form. Sheer revulsion.

'Were you ogling at me, you fool!?' Damayanti asked. 'Lucky my dog did not chew you.'

When she spoke, he stared at her, his eyes anguished. The distress was so clear that Damayanti approached him cautiously and checked for injuries. Nala's eyes filled up.

'Stop staring at me,' Damayanti snapped and Nala looked down. The injured dwarf scrambled and stood. Nala came only up to Damayanti's thighs when he stood up.

'Thankfully, none of the bites are serious. Now go away,' Damayanti said. The dwarf turned and walked away, his tiny shoulders sagging.

'Poor thing,' Damayanti said, 'It doesn't even have a cloth to cover its shame.' She sighed, feeling remorseful. 'Wait,' she called out. Then tearing another piece from her upper cloth, she said, 'Wear this and cast away that string of leaves. Cover yourself properly. And don't ever stalk women! I hope you have learnt your lesson.'

Nala turned to look at her face one last time. He slowly took the piece of cloth with trembling hands and stared at it. A drop of tear fell on it. Pressing the cloth to his face and sobbing, he walked away. For some reason Damayanti felt her heart tremble.

'Poor man,' Damayanti muttered to herself, watching him go away. She turned to Hemanga, 'I should go back to my father's home. We need to find some merchant caravan bound to Vidarbha. It is not safe to travel alone in these woods.'

'Are you giving up on him?' Hemanga asked.

'Never. I am going to my father's palace because I need men and means to search for my Nala.'

* * *

Unknown to her, at the far end of the valley, the dwarf looked back for one last time to see his beloved Damayanti. *She had not recognized him.* Noting her reaction when she saw his face had sealed Nala's determination never to see Damayanti again. He whispered, 'Wherever you are, be happy my dear. Marry someone of your class and stature. Forget this unfortunate Nishada. And forgive me if you can . . . '

17

The Search

Damayanti reached Vidarbha along with a merchant caravan they had located after a day's travel. She had convinced the chief of the caravan about the reward he would receive once he safely took her and her two strange companions—Hemanga and Amavasi—to Vidarbha.

They reached Vidarbha after a month of travel. Damayanti walked into the palace hall while her father was in council with his ministers and court officials, with her Hemanga and Amavasi trotting behind her. The council meeting stopped abruptly. All eyes were on them and Hemanga could imagine how the shock of their bedraggled presence must have inflicted on the poor king and his courtiers. After all, a dishevelled princess with no sparkling gems or ornaments on her, a golden swan, a black dog, and an obese merchant with greedy eyes was the last thing they would have expected.

'Daughter,' the king sprang up from his throne. Damayanti rushed to his arms but he shrank back. Rajguru stepped in between the father and daughter.

'Move!' Damayanti commanded to the Rajguru.

'Where is your husband?' Rajguru asked. Damayanti looked helplessly at her father expecting him to intercede.

'This is my home,' Damayanti said pressingly, arching her eyebrows and looking at her father in indignation. *Why wasn't he saying anything?* Her father's silence bewildered her.

'Home,' Rajguru scoffed, 'this is not your house any more. You chose a Nishada. His home is your home, now.'

Damayanti looked at her father. 'Didn't you know?' she asked.

'Yes, we do. Now you are a mere Nishadi. Not the queen,' Rajguru smirked. 'We knew all about what happened to your low-caste husband. But wherever he is, there you should be. That is the dharma of a virtuous wife.'

Damayanti ignored Rajguru and addressed her father, 'I don't know where Nala has gone. I want your help, father. I need help to find him.'

Still, it was the minister who responded, not her father. 'Nala! Hmm. Nala! You call your husband by his name? No wonder fate played with you,' Rajguru said aloud for the courtiers to hear. He leaned towards Damayanti and smirked, 'The low caste abandoned you, right?'

'He has not abandoned me and I have not abandoned him,' Damayanti thundered. Turning to her father, she asked quietly, 'Isn't this my home too, father?'

The king stood brooding. Hemanga was tempted to speak when his gaze fell on the shadow of the priest. *There he was! Kali.* Kali with his glowing red eyes trained at Damayanti.

'Am I not your daughter any more?' Damayanti asked. The king squirmed and looked helplessly at his guru.

Damayanti looked around hoping for support from any of the courtiers. No one came forward. Her gaze fell on Hemanga and he gestured with his head and drew her attention to Rajguru's shadow. Damayanti saw Kali lurking in it and leering at her. A determined look came to Damayanti's eyes, 'Rajguru, would you care to answer my questions?' The old man cocked an eyebrow and nodded cautiously.

'Long ago, Prajapati Daksha forbade his daughter from marrying a Chandala,' Damayanti said. Rajguru frowned, not sure where this was going. 'He did not want a son-in-law who wore tiger skin to cover his shame and adorned snakes as ornaments. He asked why his daughter should marry a man who lives in the cremation ground and dances wildly to the tune of his *damru*. After all, to marry a Chandala, the lowest of low caste, was an insult.'

'You are talking about Lord Shiva,' Rajguru exclaimed in an offended tone.

'Yes, the God of Gods. Mahadev. A Chandala. A Kirata,' Damayanti paused and looked at her father. Her father the king, as all the courtiers, squirmed. Fixing her gaze on her father, she continued, 'Sati, Daksha's daughter, defied her father and married Chandala. Advised by his guru, Daksha spurned his son-in-law. He did not invite him to a ritual sacrifice he was conducting. Sati came to her father's home defying her husband, claiming that her father's home was hers too. Daksha humiliated her like how I am being humiliated now.'

'You can't compare Lord Shiva . . .' Rajguru's face hardened.

Damayanti continued, '. . . a mere Chandala for Daksha,' she smiled, '. . . and Sati, unable to bear the humiliation heaped on her husband by her father, jumped into the sacrificial fire.' Damayanti paused. Her father's lips trembled, his eyes brimming with tears. The court listened, in rapt attention.

'And then this Chandala stormed into the arrogant Daksha's palace,' she continued. 'No priest or gurus could save Daksha. This Chandala, mad with grief and fury, destroyed Daksha's palace. He chopped off Daksha's head with his *trishul*. He performed the dance of death, the Tandav, on the embers of the burned city of Daksha, this Chandala . . .'

'Har Har Mahadev,' a few courtiers cried. Soon from the throats of many, the chant was taken. *Har Har Mahadev! Har Har Mahadev!* Hemanga could feel the electricity in the air. The palace wall shook with the cries that rose as one, like thunder.

Damayanti's recounting had touched a chord. It had stopped the fears instilled in their minds by priests like Rajguru to despise some people and grovel before others like him, based on the accident of their birth. By reminding them about the irony of their beliefs that the Supreme God they prayed to, Lord Shiva, was a Chandala, the so-called lowest of low caste, Damayanti had shown how hollow their prejudice was. Her marrying Nala, a Nishada, was no different from Sati marrying Lord Shiva.

Her father was moved. 'I am sorry daughter; this is your home. I am sorry I hesitated!' he said. He hugged her tight and showered her with kisses. Hemanga could see the shadow of Rajguru shifting, writhing like a snake that had been stamped upon. The invincible Kali had been given a punch on its face by one determined woman.

Rajguru raised his staff and the hall fell to an uneasy silence.

'My son,' the priest addressed the king in a sweet voice, 'I have nothing against your daughter. She is like a granddaughter to me. But how long would your daughter stay alone. If Nala has abandoned her . . .'

'No, he has not abandoned me,' Damayanti contested.

'Oh? So where is he now?" Rajguru smiled. Damayanti looked down.

'I am telling it for your own good, daughter. You have only two choices. If he is dead, live as a widow.'

Damayanti's face flushed in anger. 'Nala is not dead,' she snapped.

The court priest said smoothly, 'Then, he has abandoned you. In that case, choose a new husband befitting your status, this time.'

Damayanti shook her head.

Rajguru faked bewilderment to the king. 'King, she is being unreasonable,' he said. 'She is the princess of the country and, she will set a bad example.'

A deadly silence reigned the hall.

'I will abandon kingship,' the king said. Startled, Damayanti cried, 'No father.'

'I don't want to force her, Rajguru. It is for her to do the right thing,' the king said ignoring Damayanti's protest. 'Just as I don't want my daughter to set a bad example. So, it is better that I step down as a king.'

'Three months,' Damayanti cried. 'Father, give me three months. If I don't find Nala by that time, I shall choose another husband.'

There was a collective sucking of air. Hemanga knew Kali had raised the stakes. Now it would be a race against time.

'Three months,' Rajguru smiled.

From the palace tower, the bell trolled thrice marking the time of the day and the beginning of the battle between the God of misfortune and a gritty woman.

18

Bahuka

Nala kept to the Uttarajanapadha, the highway that ran from the south to the north. He found an abandoned rag near a cremation ground near the city of Ujjain and exchanged his tree bark cloth for it. Never daring to show his dreadful face in the sunlight, he mostly travelled in the night. Nala foraged for leftovers near temples or wayside taverns and slept under trees. When it rained, he crawled under a rock or a stone bridge often sharing the shelter with swine and street dogs.

He was surprised to find that he was not the only one who lived or travelled in this fashion. It was as if another whole universe revealed itself when one had the eyes to see it. There were many destitute communities moving about and living in the periphery. Many were proscribed by caste rules to never show their faces in broad sunlight. Even their shadows were considered polluting. They had to carry a broom tied to their back to sweep their polluting footmarks from the path.

The world he had descended to was fiercer than the one he had left behind. In the city, men fought for power, money, and women, and here in the dark bellies of this netherworld, men fought for survival. Life was putrid here and men scurried like rodents. Nala understood that there was no poetry in this netherworld. The poets who romanticized the virtues of the rustic life had never lived in its forgotten corners. The villages were cesspits of tribalism and caste. Nala was seeing life with all its claws and fangs bared. In the shadows of glorious temples and palaces, lay the pits of putrid minds. Cursed were those, who, by accident of birth, had been born in the wrong wombs. Crueller was the fate of those who were born differently. The dwarf, the blind, the mute, the dumb, the malformed, men who were trapped in a woman's body and vice versa, all who did not conform to the unimaginative verses in holy books written by mad men, were crushed mercilessly like ants in the path of a marching elephant. These were the jungles of Kali. Nala was a dwarf now and that was a crime.

And he walked like a thief, keeping to the shadows. Some who prided themselves to be kind would fling some food at him and watch him eat with smug satisfaction of their noble nature.

After stumbling through jungles, skirting around nondescript villages and congested towns, Nala found asylum with a group of pilgrims going to the holy city of Varanasi. A big city like Varanasi was what he wanted. He could hide in its winding lanes or find refuge among mendicants who lived on the cremation ghats. In a city where people flocked to die, life would be easier, he decided. No one would care for his ugliness.

It was a pilgrim caravan consisting of rich merchants going to the holy city of Shiva. They were weary of the world and were trying out a life of detachment. They were disposing off their wealth by giving it away and flinging coins at the poor. A train of destitute followed the pilgrim caravan, fighting like hungry dogs for their coins. Sometimes they would feed the poor.

It was in one of such charity feeding by the pilgrims that the head of the caravan noticed Nala. He saw the dwarf was sniffing the curry poured over his heap of rice and wrinkling his nose in distaste. It enraged the head pilgrim that a beggar had frowned on the food he had given as charity.

Next thing he knew, Nala found himself standing before the chief of the caravan, Suvarnagupta. The chief asked in a sarcastic tone, 'Swami, it seems the food did not agree with you,' Nala did not reply. He stood staring at his toes, 'Answer me,' Suvarnagupta snapped.

Nala slowly raised his eyes and said, 'The dish was undercooked.'

Suvarnagupta stared at him, 'How audacious of you to comment on free food, beggar!'

'The food was bad. If you feed the poor for divine merit, you should feed them properly,' Nala responded calmly.

Suvarnagupta glared at him, 'If I wasn't on a pilgrimage, I would have had you whipped.'

'This is not how a dish is to be cooked,' Nala said, unfazed. 'If you allow me, I can show you.'

The merchant burst out in laughter, 'You think we will eat what you cook?'

'I thought the purpose of this pilgrimage is to see God in everything. It is to make you think that you are Shiva, and I am too. Yet you are still thinking in terms of who is pure and who is not,' Nala scoffed, 'What is the use of your pilgrimage?'

Suvarnagupta was taken aback. He sat in silence for some moments.

'Go and wash yourself, dwarf. I shall make arrangements for you to prepare us some dish.'

* * *

Walking to the river to bathe, Nala wondered what had prompted him to provoke the old man. He had never cooked anything for a long time. He had lost his will to do anything. Every moment, he pined for Damayanti. What had made him frown at the taste of the charity food? Was it the proof that his *kama*, the passion for life had not died and was only hidden like embers under the ash of his unhappiness? He would cook the dish for the pilgrims and run away in the morning, thought Nala.

However, when he started cooking, he forgot that he hated life. Before the eyes of the astonished merchants, he started chopping meat and vegetables with a dexterity that would have shamed a master chef. When he ground the spices and their aroma spread, people stopped whatever they were doing to draw long breaths. When the dish started bubbling up in the stove, men had already spread banana leaves in anticipation. Even the people from other pilgrim camps started coming in to enquire what was cooking and jostled for space in the dining camp.

Suvarnagupta put the first morsel in his mouth and just forgot himself. Flavours and textures of all kinds exploded in his mouth, with the very first bite. He opened his eyes and saw the dwarf before him. Tears rolled down the old man's cheeks. 'You are unbelievable,' he said. In the dining hall, men were literally fighting for Nala's savouries.

Then looking, really looking, at the dwarf who had created such perfection, Suvarnagupta smiled at him and asked, 'What is your name, son?'

Nala blurted out the first name that came to his mind, 'Bahuka.'

'Bahuka? Strange name,' Suvarnagupta remarked. 'What God has denied you in stature, he has lavished you in culinary skills. Your cooking could start a war, little man.'

19

The Plan

Damayanti sent spies far and wide to find Nala. Each carried a painting of Nala that Damayanti had made. While Rajguru counted days for the three months to end, King Bhimasena declared a reward of one lakh gold coins for anyone who would give any information about his son-in-law.

Hemanga was conducting his own search. He could fly far and wide and was confident that he could be swifter than any spy or informer of King Bhimasena. Time was running out. By the end of the second month, Hemanga started fearing that something bad had happened to Nala. Yet, he refused to give up hope.

An idea started forming in his mind. It involved Amavasi. Hemanga flew to the Nishada kingdom. He hid himself in the half-finished temple in the Nishada land for four days. He learned many things: Pushkara was the king of a namesake. Swami Dvapara was now the prime minister and held all the power. He had brought in his friends and they held all the important positions in the country. The old and trusted aides of Nala had either been killed or jailed. Now, men who were once street artists and monkey dancers a few months ago were the ones running the land as ministers. The newcomers declared themselves as superior to the Nishadas and soon the Nishadas had no permission to walk in the streets of the city, drink from public well, or stroll in the gardens. They could not even enter the temples. They had been rendered untouchable. People looked back at the reign of Nala as the golden age, but new teachers who made stories about how arrogant Nala was and why Gods had to punish him had arrived and were busy with the intent of creating new narratives.

Hemanga had arrived to this new Nishada land. He sneaked into the sleeping chamber of Pushkara and tiptoed around the bed and saw what he had come for. Dangling on the armchair of the cushioned chair by the window was a shawl, Nala's uthariya made of the finest gold threads. He pulled it from the chair. It had a faint scent of Nala. Hemanga started rolling it into a ball. Pushkara stirred in his sleep and turned to one side. His hand hit Hemanga's head and the bird gave a squeak of pain. Pushkara opened his eyes and stared at Hemanga. The bird froze with fear. The shawl he had rolled into a ball fell and rolled on the floor.

'You!' Pushkara sprang up. Hemanga swooped the shawl with his beak and shot out of the window. Pushkara lunged at him and got hold of one end of the gold shawl. Hemanga tucked the other end with all his might. Both were determined. Pushkara cussed and yelled, Hemanga flapped his wings, desperate to take the shawl and escape. He knew the ruckus was sure to wake up the palace and soon the Nishadas would be after him, hurling stones and shooting arrows.

'Shame on you to harry a poor bird like me,' Hemanga cried. A loud crash was followed by a string of cuss words. Hemanga had inadvertently let go of the shawl to curse Pushkara. The king lost his balance and toppled on the floor. Dazed and disoriented, he sat spread-legged on the floor with the shawl lying limp over his head. Hemanga seized the opportunity, flew in, scooped the shawl, and quickly flew his way out. He could see Pushkara at the window, shaking his fist and baying for Hemanga's blood. The bird braced for a volley of arrows. When he looked down, he saw a few Nishadas staring at him with vacant expression in the palace courtyard. They looked wearily at their livid king gesticulating from the palace window, but they did nothing. That was a measure of how unpopular Pushkara had become.

Hemanga sighed in relief and hurried to Vidarbha. The first step of his plan had succeeded.

20

Kidnapped

Nala was kidnapped near the banks of the Sarayu river. His reputation as a great culinary expert had made the caravan swell with newcomers. Nala was exhausted by the continuous cooking of delicious meals. The pilgrims decided to take a circuitous route to Kashi as no one wanted the delicious feast of Nala to end. They were often waylaid by other merchant caravans who had heard about the famous cook of Suvarnagupta. Many offered huge sums of money in exchange for the master chef, Bahuka.

Suvarnagupta pompously declared, 'He is not a mere servant. Bahuka is my brother from another mother.'

The fame of Nala spread far and wide. Soon kings started arriving, offering Suvarnagupta huge sums of money. Suvarnagupta denied every offer. He stopped free meals and started charging for each dish Nala cooked. Charity was soon forgotten. There was no time for God now. Money flowed in like the river Ganga into Suvarnagupta's coffers. Kashi too was forgotten. Who wanted to think of moksha when delicious payasam was waiting for them?

On the outskirts of Ayodhya, a hulky man visited Suvarnagupta once. He ate the sumptuous feast cooked by the dwarf Bahuka and belched in satisfaction. When he finished, the giant offered a great treasure if only Suvarnagupta would part with his cook.

Suvarnagupta said, 'Bahuka's family had been serving us as cooks for many generations. He is a family heirloom, gifted by my father to me on his death bed. I would sell my head, but not Bahuka, the precious.'

The giant old man did not press his offer further. That night, while Nala was sleeping after an exhaustive day's work, a blanket fell over him. Before he could even cry out, he found himself trussed in it and being carried away. He was dropped unceremoniously into a wooden board and then he heard paddles hitting the water. He was on a boat. Nala had no idea who had kidnapped him and why. Was Kali still playing this game? The boat reached the shore, and he was soon being carried on someone's shoulders.

After some time, they unwrapped him and he found he was inside a luxurious palace. The silk curtains, the polished floor, glided furniture, and the soft carpets bespoke of a luxury unaffordable by lesser mortals. An exquisitely carved peacock sat on the crest of a golden lamp and stared at him with its ruby eyes. In a corner, a silver bowl was emitting fragrant smoke.

The door flung open startling him and a train of maidens walked in. Ignoring his protests, they washed him and made him wear garments of the finest silk. An elderly woman wrapped a gold-laced shawl around his shoulders. She applied a red mark on his forehead and observed him at an arm's length.

'Perfect,' she said with a smile, and spat a stream of beetle juice to a golden spittoon held by her assistant.

'What is the meaning of all these?" Nala asked.

'You are getting married,' the old woman said, and her companions burst into laughter. They marched Nala through the winding corridors of the palace. They made snide remarks about his indignant expressions and giggled at his every move. The procession wound through a maze of halls and corridors. In the flickering light of torches, Nala could see amusement in the eyes of the soldiers who stood guard on the corridors as the procession went by. From balconies, women ogled at him. Conscious of his ugliness and the ridiculous costume he was wearing, Nala felt miserable.

He was weary of the hands of fate that were making him play the role of a jester. He walked listlessly wondering what more Kali had in store for him. Damayanti's smiling face flashed in his mind and it took all his self-control to not burst into tears. The procession stopped in front of a closed door. The head woman whispered something in the ears of the doorkeeper and pointed at Nala.

'He looks hideous,' the doorkeeper said.

'He has not come seeking your daughter's hand in marriage. It is king's orders. Open the door, you fool,' the old woman said. With distaste, the guard opened the door. Nala knew the effect his hideous face had on people the first time they looked at it. *This was the price he had paid for helping a snake.* Yet he had no regrets. He knew that had he not saved the snake he would have lost his sleep forever.

Like a grandma leading her grandchild to the guru, the woman led Nala into the brightly lit room. He heard a collective sucking of air. When his eyes adjusted to the golden hewed brightness of the room, he could see many men and women sitting and standing with crystal goblets of a sparkling liquid in their hands. The diamonds in their ornaments sparkled and their silk clothes shimmered when they moved. A table with an array of gold plates and bowls was set in the middle of the hall. At the far end sat a huge man.

The ruby in his turban was as big as a mango. With a chest full of ornaments and a purple silk dress, he sat on a peacock throne with an amiable smile. Nala had seen him before. He was the one who had offered a stupendous price for buying him from Suvarnagupta.

'This is Bahuka, the greatest cook in the world,' the bulky man stood up and said with a wide grin. Nala looked at him again. He was really huge. All the courtiers looked at Nala. Everyone started clapping.

'Come my brother, embrace me,' the man said, spreading his arms far and wide. Nala walked towards him reluctantly and the applause grew louder. Nala was conscious of everyone's stares. *They all see my ugly face*, he thought bitterly.

'What is he cooking for us today?' someone yelled. Many cried out their choices in response. When Nala reached the huge man, he bent forward to wrap Nala in a bear hug.

'Uff!' A groan escaped Nala's mouth as he felt all his bones creaking beneath the man's powerful, crushing hug.

'Welcome to the palace of King Rituparna, the monarch of Ayodhya,' his voice boomed. Nala struggled to smile.

'In case you are wondering who is Rituparna in this crowd, don't look farther,' the giant guffawed. After a dramatic pause, he said. 'It is me,' and exploded with laughter. Everyone took the cue and laughed. The palace walls trembled as laughter swept in waves through the hall.

'My king, how much did you pay for him?' a woman asked fluttering her long eyelashes.

'Devi, I got him for free.'

'Free?' the guests cried.

'I stole him,' Rituparna slapped Nala's back and laughed.

The coterie laughed with him. 'Stole him! Stole him!' they chanted, amused.

'You are such a hero,' another woman cried.

'Bah,' Rituparna said dismissively, 'Who wants to be a hero? My dynasty has enough heroes. Poets are bored of writing about their heroism. Let us sing and dance.'

The crowd cheered and whistled. Servants ran to fill each chalice. The king grabbed a huge pot of Soma sap and tipped it down his throat. The crowd cheered his performance. Rituparna wiped the froth from his haggard salt and pepper beard, belched loudly, and rubbed his potbelly. 'Eat, drink, and enjoy. That is the way to live. Maharishi Charvaka, the good fellow said, eat drink, and enjoy. Tomorrow we may die, live life on a high. Who knows whether there are Gods?'

Perhaps this had been announced before because the crowd answered with practised ease and in unison: 'Who cares where is heaven?'

Rituparna boomed again, 'There is no tomorrow, there is no yesterday.'

'Not even today,' they filled in. 'There is only now.'

Rituparna answered, 'Live for now.' He cleared his throat and sang in a loud voice.' Ask the priests who croak mantras . . .'

'. . . to jump into the waters of Ganga.' His courtiers knew it by heart. They chanted in unison, 'Live for today, live for this moment.'

Rituparna sang: Forget all woes and kick fate in its face,

Who cares what lies beyond death?
Some priests say, there is heaven,
Waiting for the virtuous with open gates
They say the pits of hell lay in wait
For those who spurn their words
No one has seen it, heaven or hell
Yet, they speak big words and croak like frogs

Some scholars threaten us, O sinners,
There is life after death and death
After life, again and again and again
To be born as a swine, as a man,
As a woman, as both, as a bird or a beast
As a tree or grass and suffer your fate
Tell them no one cares,
As long as we are born
Again, and again and again
In this beautiful world
Who will tell them, there is no sin?
There is, no virtue, no right, no wrong,
No hero, no villain, no God, no demon
This earth is a fancy stage, life a play
Rules are simple, there are no rules
Laugh when happy, cry when sad
Dance with joy, fight with passion
Love thyself, love life and love death
Live and love and live for now
Here and now. Now, now. Now.

'We are here, now. Eat, drink, and enjoy.' The uproar ended with a burst of laughter, hoots, and whistles. Nala did not know what had changed but a sudden spurt of vigour ran down his spine. *This was a room where Kali could not enter.* The God of misfortune had no power among those who lived here and now.

Rituparna leaned towards Nala and said with a smile, 'Now my brother Bahuka, treat us with your blessed art.'

Nala bowed and proceeded to the royal kitchen. The first sight of it took his breath away. In a massive hall, there were rows of stoves and huge vessels on them. Men stood waiting for his orders and they bowed to him in respect. For the first time since he had parted from Damayanti, Nala smiled. The power of the moment filled his veins. From the hall, the laughter of Rituparna echoed. Nala started preparing his first dish for Rituparna.

21

The Spy

Amavasi sniffed the golden shawl Hemanga had brought and started running. Damayanti followed the dog on her horse. By noon, after many detours and water breaks, the tired dog reached the bush where Damayanti had met Hemanga a few months ago. The dog got excited and started barking, sniffing and running around the bush where the dwarf had hidden.

Damayanti and Hemanga looked at each other, 'Maybe, the dwarf knew something about Nala,' Hemanga said.

Damayanti sniffled a sob, 'I am scared, the dwarf looked so evil. I still remember his face. Would he have harmed Nala?'

'No, no, don't lose hope,' Hemanga said, as Amavasi shot towards the north, and they followed. They soon reached the swift-flowing Narmada and the trail ended there, 'The dwarf has crossed the river here, I need to look for him in the northern kingdoms.' Then bowing to Damayanti, the swan said, 'I will find the dwarf somehow, someone would remember. His ugly face was remarkable and not so easy to forget.'

Saying goodbye, Hemanga flew north.

Two weeks later he got the first hint. In a tavern near the city of Vaishali, he heard about the strange appearance and disappearance of an ugly dwarf whose fame in cooking had made him precious. Some said he was some goblin or evil spirit who used magic for cooking. The reference to the cooking skill of the dwarf made Hemanga sit up and notice. What he suspected for some time now, was turning to be true. *The dwarf had pressed the rag to his face*! The tenderness in his eyes when he looked at the gift of Damayanti had touched Hemanga. Now, he was almost certain of the reason: the dwarf was no evil goblin but Nala.

Where had he vanished again? Hemanga continued his inquiry without pausing to rest. Three days later he saw a group of Brahmins hurrying towards the ancient city of Ayodhya. They were talking about the delicious feast that awaited them. One of the Brahmins who had tasted the food earlier was enticing his companions with its description.

'The king of Ayodhya may not be the pious type,' the Brahmin told his companion, kissing the tips of his fingers fervently, 'but he feeds all who pass through his city and what a feast he holds! There is a rumour that he has trapped a *bhoota* that makes delicious food. And the bhoota is a dwarf.'

Without wasting time, Hemanga soared to Ayodhya. As he reached the palace, he could hear the roar of the milling crowds. Servants were hurrying with humongous vessels hanging from poles perched on their shoulders. Steaming dishes spread a heavenly aroma in the air and the crowd jostled for more. The huge figure of Rituparna could be seen at the terrace of the palace. The king waved at the excited crowd and bellowed, 'Eat, drink, and enjoy. There is no heaven or hell. Enjoy your life, now.'

The crowd did not care either way. Who wants to debate about God or his absence when a delicious feast was waiting? 'More, more, give us more!' the crowd chanted. The more they ate the more they wanted. Rituparna laughed at the avarice of the crowd. He pointed at a gang of mendicants who were knocking each other's heads with their staff.

'Look Bahuka, what evil have you done?' Rituparna laughed, 'Woohaahaa . . . I am loving this. Those are the men who had given up everything in life to know about Brahman. They were in search of the absolute truth, whatever that may be. Now they are ready to kill for some food. What fun!' Rituparna laughed and yelled at his servants, 'Give them more of those laddoos! Tell them there is enough for everyone and we will make more if needed. Let them not kill each other. Bahuka will make more!'

But the mendicants were in no mood to listen. The crowd jostled, pushed, shoved and kicked, even abused, and broke heads and limbs for more. 'Look at those fools. Each of them wants everything for himself, whether something is useful or not, or whether he has enough of it or not. If a neighbour has more, they want more than more. Nothing is more intolerable than other people's happiness,' Rituparna hollered.

Hemanga saw a little man standing by the side of the king. Now he was left with no doubts. The hideous-looking dwarf was Nala. Tucked in his silk waistband was the torn piece of cloth that Damayanti had gifted. It was prudent to stay hidden from Nala's view, thought Hemanga. After all, Nala had not chosen to reveal himself when they had last met. Hemanga did not want him to vanish again.

Little did Hemanga know that he need not have worried. There was nowhere that Nala could vanish. He was a prisoner of Rituparna.

The roar of the crowd jostling to grab a fistful of laddoos reached a crescendo now. It felt like riots were breaking out in the city. Rituparna was, however, undaunted by it. In fact, he was enjoying every moment of it.

Nala asked Rituparna, 'Why aren't you breaking this? They are fighting for my laddoos.'

Rituparna laughed, saying, 'The fools will find some reason or another to fight. Isn't it better that they fight for laddoos instead of fighting in the name of some God or a few lines in some holy book? At least, the winner would have some laddoo in this life instead of empty promises about the life after death.'

Hemanga, who had been quietly eavesdropping, had heard enough. He quickly realized that Nala was now in the captivity of an eccentric old man, which meant there was no way he would be able to reunite him with Damayanti before the designated time. His mission to save the human race was now thwarted not by Kali but an affable half-mad king who wanted nothing more than good food, wine, and laughter.

'Die, you fools,' Hemanga hissed. 'Let you all be wiped clean off the face of this earth and let Brahma make the reptiles the masters of the world again.'

Hemanga decided that he should inform Damayanti about what he had found; that he should take some proof for her to believe Nala was in Ayodhya. He scanned to see what that proof could be.

A man, who had successfully fought his rivals and won his prize, was about to drop the sweet into his open mouth while keeping a bunch of bickering rivals away at an arm's length with his other hand. Hemanga swooped in and snatched it from his mouth and in the next instant shot upward to the sky, leaving the angry man shaking his fists at him in fury. The men he had beaten moments before, erupted in howls of laughter at his misfortune and went to fight elsewhere.

Holding his precious parcel between his beak, relieved he had something, Hemanga left the fools far behind and sped towards Vidarbha. It took all his will not to gobble up the sweet himself for its delicious aroma was so tempting.

* * *

He presented the laddoo to Damayanti. She broke a piece of the sweetmeat and put it in her mouth. She closed her eyes savouring its delicious flavours and then burst into tears. No words were exchanged. No words were needed to be exchanged. The laddoo was clearly the creation of Nala.

'Where is he?' she asked. When Hemanga finished narrating how he met Nala, Damayanti closed her eyes in deep thought.

'I don't know how that king is ever going to free his favourite cook,' Hemanga said. 'From what I heard and saw, it felt as if he may give up his kingdom but not Nala. Even if he frees Nala by some fortune, there are only three days now for your time to end.'

Damayanti opened her eyes and smiled at him, 'What if we make Rituparna bring him here?'

'How?' Hemanga cried. When Damayanti told what she had in mind, Hemanga said, 'But it is too risky, Devi, and there is no way they can reach in such a short time. It is a week's journey from here unless they can fly like me.

'You don't know Nala,' Damayanti said. She picked up a cloth roll from her bed. She unrolled it to show a marvellous painting of herself. At the back of it, she hurriedly scribbled a letter. 'That is an invitation from my father Bhimasena, the King of Vidarbha,' she said rolling it back and handing it over to Hemanga.

'For what?' Hemanga asked.

'For the swayamvara of his daughter Damayanti four days from now.'

'Are you crazy?' Hemanga cried.

'If that does not bring Nala . . .' Damayanti did not finish the sentence. She turned away from him, 'I am going to tell my father that I am ready for remarriage. If Nala wants me, he should come here in three days.' And with that Damayanti hurried out to hide her anguish. The door slammed shut.

Only a miracle could save the couple, thought the bird as he flew back to Ayodhya with the invitation for Damayanti's swayamvara.

22

The Party

There was singing and dancing as usual in Ayodhya when Hemanga reached. The sky was greying in the east yet the merriment in the dining hall of Rituparna's palace had just started. Exhausted with non-stop flying, without taking even a second for a water break, Hemanga could barely stand. He perched on the roof of the palace, then holding the painting roll with his foot, he removed a tile from the roof and peered down. The music and the charged laughter hit him. Rituparna, dressed like a dandy, was strutting around, with a crystal of Soma rasa in his hand.

'Let us now sing an ode to Soma,' Rituparna said, jiving with the music, and the crowd cheered. 'An ode to Soma, from Rig Veda.'

'Ode to Soma, the great drink of Gods!' the crowd cheered him on.

'Am I not drunk on Soma juice?' Rituparna crooned.

'Like winds, so wild, its draughts lifting me,' sang a man from the other end. The crowd cheered.

'Am I not drunk on Soma juice?'

Then they sang in unison. 'The draughts of Soma is dragging me, as steads draw a cart!'

'Am I not drunk on Soma juice? . . .'

And, on and on it went. The refrain spun from a single line, with each response adding to the intoxication and the high of the drink, the music, and the camaraderie.

'This hymn of the ancients has come to me, like a cow who yearns to meet her darling calf.'

'Like a cow, like a cow, like a cow to meet its darling calf.'

'Am I not drunk on Soma juice?'

'The heavens and earth themselves have not grown equal to one half of me.'

'Am I not drunk on Soma juice?'

'I have surpassed the heavens and all this spacious earth.'

'Yes, I have, I have, I have.'

'Am I not drunk on Soma juice?'

'I am, I am, I am.'

'Aha! Where should I deposit this huge earth?'

'Here, there, wherever.'

'Am I not drunk on Soma juice?'

'I am, I am, I am.'

'In my fury, where I shall kick this earth?'

'There, here, wherever.'

'Am I not drunk on Soma juice?'

'I am, I am, I am.'

'The earth is above, the sky is below, one hand is there, and one hand is here.'

'Am I not drunk on Soma juice?'

'An ode to the drink of Gods.'

'I am the God, where are my worshippers, where is my abode?'

'Here, here, heaven is here, where Soma is.'

'I am, I am, I am the God.'

'Am I not drunk on Soma juice?

'An ode to the drink of Gods.'

Men and women were dancing and Rituparna ambled around like a performing elephant in their midst. Hemanga saw Nala standing in a corner, between two soldiers guarding him, a picture of misery. Whenever Rituparna passed Nala, he would cry, 'Bahuka, my dear friend, life is short. Don't just stand there and watch it pass by. Come and enjoy with us.'

Hemanga lifted the painting scroll with his beak and dropped it down. He watched with bated breath as it spiralled and landed near Nala. The dwarf picked it up and looked up. Colour drained off Nala's face as he caught a glimpse of Hemanga. With trembling hands, he unrolled it and stared at Damayanti's smiling face. Even from high above, Hemanga could see Nala's lips tremble and his hands shake. The painting fell from his hands. It rolled towards the dance floor and got kicked around by many feet. With a cry of anguish, Nala rushed to retrieve it. Every time he tried to pick it up, a dancer's feet would kick it unintentionally away from his reach. Rituparna saw Nala in the dancing ring and gave a whoop of joy.

'That is the way, my little friend. Welcome.' He rushed to Nala and lifted him up. The crowd cheered and said in unison, 'Welcome, Bahuka. Welcome, good dwarf!'

They applauded, and the dance became, if that was even possible, more frantic.

Hemanga was desperate and thought of diving down to retrieve the scroll, when a young woman picked it up. Curious, she moved to the light of a wall torch and started reading it.

She exclaimed, 'This is an invitation for swayamvara.' She waved the roll at Rituparna. 'Your Highness, an invitation for you.' Rituparna raised his hand and the music stopped. He gently put Nala on the floor. The woman read the invitation aloud. Hemanga saw Nala's face glistening with tears. His world had collapsed around him, again. Though he had always insisted

Damayanti should forget him and marry another, the news of her swayamvara shattered him. Hemanga held his breath.

'Why should I bother about another marriage? I have seven wives already and each of them is trouble,' the king said, and the hall reverberated with raucous laughter. One of his queens punched his belly and the king guffawed, leading to more laughter.

'Well, let me see whether this will change your mind,' the woman, teasing him, said, and with deliberate slowness, turned the message over to reveal Damayanti's painting.

The crowd gasped. Rituparna stared at it for a moment and exclaimed, 'What a beauty!' He hurried to the woman and snatched it from her hand to have a closer look. His friends crowded over his shoulders, and the room filled with the talk about her beauty. In one corner, forgotten by everyone, Nala stood silently crying.

'Bah!' Rituparna's voice startled Hemanga who had been looking at Nala. The king flung the painting on the floor. 'Three days from today. I can never reach Vidarbha by that time. Who brought this message so late?'

A man cried, 'Let us catch that lazy messenger and have him whipped.'

'Hah! Let us not waste time worrying about what can't be helped. Let the beautiful maiden marry whoever she chooses. We have no time to waste. Let the party continue,' Rituparna said, gesturing to his musicians to resume playing.

Nala cried aloud, 'Your highness, if we start now, we can reach Vidarbha just in time.' All heads turned towards him, Rituparna walked to him and bent towards the dwarf to level with his face.

'Did you tip the wine down your throat while we were not looking? It is a seven-day journey, my friend,' Rituparna said and smiled.

'I will take you in two,' Nala cried.

'How? Are we going to fly?' Rituparna asked, flapping his stubby arms.

Nala waited for the laughter in the hall to die down. Then he turned on his heels and marched out. On the way, he picked up the painting from the floor. A curious Rituparna followed and the others marched behind. Nala walked to a chariot in the courtyard. The horses leaned towards him, he chanted something in their ears and jumped in. He sat on the driver's seat and took the reins.

'Well,' the mighty-sized king smiled, 'let us entertain my little friend.' The king climbed into the chariot and waved at his admirers. He had not even completed his gesture, when the chariot shot forward like lightning.

'Hey! Hey!' Rituparna cried struggling to keep his balance as the chariot careened at the fort gate and raced through the royal highway, leaving a cloud of dust. Hemanga gave a whoop of joy and yelled at the astonished onlookers who were staring at the road where the chariot had vanished.

'Go and dance, you fools.' If their king being carried away in a lightning-fast chariot had not startled them, a talking bird certainly did. They scrambled to get inside, screaming in terror, while some others ran out, desperate to reach their homes, certain that the Soma juice they had been drinking all night long had made them hallucinate. A talking bird indeed. Who was going to believe them in the morning?

23

Three Gods Again

'Oh boy! That was exhilarating and nerve-wracking. Rituparna yelled over the din of the rattling chariot. They had travelled relentlessly from Ayodhya with Hemanga perched on the canopy of the chariot. As the chariot passed the city gate of Vidarbha, they could feel the festivity in the air.

Every home was decorated with garlands of hibiscus and lotus flowers. Festoons hung across the streets. Women were drawing rangoli and the street was filled with musicians and bards. Chariots of various princes from across lands rattled by, capricious elephants carrying kings ambled past with their hired poets singing paeans about their master's propensity in art and bravery in the war, in proportion to the fees they had received.

'This is so wonderful,' Rituparna exclaimed. 'We came in a hurry. Else, we also could have brought some bards to sing about my achievements: drinking forty-eight vases of Soma rasa at one go.' The king guffawed at his own wit, but Nala was not smiling. He looked deathly pale. King Bhimasena came out to receive them. He praised the humility of Rituparna. Unlike other kings and princes who had come with huge paraphernalia, Rituparna, the scion of an illustrious kingdom like Ayodhya, had come with one servant and that too a dwarf.

'Ha, ha, I don't even have a dress to change,' Rituparna said, sniffing his uthariya that reeked of Soma rasa and wrinkling his own nose in distaste.

'Everything will be taken care of, your highness,' smiled King Bhimasena and led them to their guestrooms. Hemanga flew behind them, hoping to catch a moment in private with Nala and convince him to somehow meet Damayanti.

'Bahuka, my friend, do you have my pair of dices with you by any chance?' Rituparna asked as soon as they had settled in the rooms. From afar, the sound of dice rolling on board could be heard. Some people were obviously playing the game of dyuta. Nala shook his head and Rituparna swore. 'I think I have to play with their pair of dices.'

Rituparna hurried to the far end of the corridor and Nala followed. Hemanga looked around and tiptoed on his feet behind them. At the far end of the corridor, a door was half open and a rectangle of lamplight fell on the floor through the crack. Rituparna pushed open the door and said, 'Namaskar friends.' The room went silent. Rituparna walked in, oblivious of the cold reception he had received.

Hemanga standing in the shadows a few feet behind craned his neck to see who the players were.

'I am the King of Ayodhya. Oh, you are only three playing the game of dyuta. Shall I join as the fourth player?' Hemanga shuddered. *He knew who the three young men were.* Indra, the King of Gods. Agni, the God of fire, and Yama, the God of death. Indra watched Rituparna with amusement.

'We are four,' Yama said.

'Have you got tipsy so early in the evening, young man?' Rituparna chuckled and took the empty place. The Gods were not lying. Hemanga knew the fourth place was taken by the invisible Kali. A shadow shifted as Rituparna pulled the empty stool and plonked his heavy frame on it. Hemanga could see two red eyes glowering at Rituparna from the shadows. Without even being aware of it, Rituparna had expelled Kali so nonchalantly.

Rituparna looked at the board with interest and said, 'Interesting positions. I am afraid, I haven't got my pair of dice. So, you have to kindly lend me yours.'

Indra was amused of this huge amiable old man. He said, 'Anything you ask for, Swami.'

'You said it, boy,' Rituparna's laughter boomed. 'Kings should be like that. If someone asks, we should give without a second thought. We did not bring anything when we were born, and we shall have no use of anything when we are gone.'

'But, we don't die,' said Agni.

'One day everyone will. By the way, young man, which kingdom do you each rule?'

'I am the God of heavens,' Indra said.

Rituparna stared at him and then his entire body shook in mirth. 'God of heaven, ho, ho, ho! You are so witty. Just because your mother has put your name as that of the King of Gods, do you think you are really that chap?' Rituparna slapped Indra on his back and Indra winced. 'Where have you parked your white elephant, son? Why are you staring at me? Haven't you heard the funny tale that poets have made about heavens. There is this bloke called Indra, your namesake, who is the King of Gods as per this fantastic tale. He has a white elephant. Well, every king has one or a few of them who pretend to work. Some call themselves courtiers, some call themselves officials. Pests. I too have many. But this guy has a real white tusker which has four tusks as per storytellers. Good imagination, I say. They should have added wings to the elephant too. And this guy has many nymphs in his court to entertain him. Rambha, Menaka, Urvashi, Thilottama and so on. My kind of guy, this Indra chap. Are you related to him?'

'Second cousin,' offered Indra and got three slaps on his back as reward for his wit.

Rituparna turned to Agni, 'And you, young man?'

'He is in charge of the fire,' Yama said.

Rituparna looked at Agni and at Indra, 'You don't say!'

'Yes, he is.'

'How wonderful.' Rituparna addressed Indra. 'I love the way you treat your servants.'

'Servants?' Agni choked in rage.

'You are his cook, aren't you?' Rituparna asked.

'He cooks a lot,' Indra said before Agni could reply. Agni glowered at Indra, who was bursting with laughter. Even Yama had a smile.

Rituparna said, 'It is nice of you to treat your cook as your equal. Is it always like this or is it only when you are drunk and start imagining that you are the King of Gods?'

It was Yama's turn to laugh aloud. Rituparna turned to him, 'And you, young man?'

'He takes care of buffaloes,' Agni said with a smile of revenge.

'Buffalos? Oh, you are his herdsman! I see. Do you milk them?' Rituparna asked in admiration. Yama decided a dignified silence would be the apt reply.

'You should see him travelling atop his buffalo. He looks deadly,' Agni added with a sweet smile. Yama's face had shrunk. He said in a menacing voice. 'I am the lord of death.'

'Of buffaloes?' Rituparna asked. 'You skin them after they are dead? A butcher?' Now it was Indra and Agni who were laughing their heads off.

'I am time, Kaala,' Yama said in a grave voice.

Rituparna stared at him for a moment and shook his head in dismay, 'Boy, you are stoned.'

'I am time,' Yama's voice was desperate. 'I am known as Kaala.'

'Then I am season. I am Ritu.' Rituparna hollered and slapped Yama's thighs. Indra and Agni were howling with laughter. 'You are remarkable, my king, have you come with your son for swayamvara?'

'Son?' Rituparna's face flushed with embarrassment. That is not my son, he is my friend. A great cook. Master chef Bahuka.'

The three Gods looked at the dwarf. From behind Rituparna, Kali laughed. Rituparna turned back. There was no one there and the old king became uneasy. 'Who is laughing behind my back?'

'Oh, no one,' Indra said reassuringly. 'We did not ask about this ugly dwarf. He can't be your son. You are so handsome. We asked, oh . . .' Indra stared at him and said, 'if you have come as a contestant?'

'Well, why not?' Rituparna asked with a sheepish smile.

'Oh nothing,' Agni said placidly.

'You are too old and fat,' Yama growled, still smarting from the irreverence he had faced from the old king.

Rituparna's bulky hand shot out and grabbed Yama by his neck. He slammed the God of death to the wall, 'Who is fat, you buffalo man? How dare you insult a king? I will kill you.'

'Don't, don't,' Indra cried.

Agni hollered, 'Oh I can't wait to tell this to our friends. Vayu is going to be breathless with laughter.'

Indra pulled Rituparna back and the old man stood panting, still angry at Yama who was rasping to catch his breath.

'You almost ruined the world,' Indra said. 'If you kill death, then no one can die.'

Rituparna cried, 'You all are talking nonsense. How can I kill death? For death to die, death should live, right? And if death lives, how can death die?'

'Not even Brahma can answer that,' Indra said.

'Young man, I thought I could play a game of dice with you. When young men start discussing philosophy instead of girls and bullfights, they are too drunk to be of any use. We will meet another day,' Rituparna turned to go.

'One day we will play dice against each other and then you will wish that you were never born,' Kali hissed.

Rituparna turned back scowling, 'Who is talking behind my back, who is there to challenge me?'

'The God of misfortune, the God of fate, Kali,' said Yama. 'Don't challenge him.'

'Fate, God,' Rituparna laughed. 'There is nothing called fate or God. If I am not afraid of tomorrow or worry about yesterday, why should I bother about these old wives' tales about Gods and fate? Buffalo man, cook and—what did you say you were? Hah, the King of Gods. I will give you a simple law to live life. Eat, drink, and make merry. Life is too short. Live as if you are going to die the next moment and live as if you are going to live forever. No fate can touch you and you need no God, heaven, or hell other than what you make in your mind. Goodnight, young man.' Rituparna marched out holding Nala's hand.

Indra, Agni, and Yama watched him with admiration. 'If all humans become like him, then we would be irrelevant,' said Indra. A howl rose from the shadows, 'You can all go to your world, you lucky ones. I am cursed to be on earth. I was created by humans. If they do not fear me, what will happen to me? I want Brahma to annihilate the humans, so that I can come with you.'

'Oh, don't worry, brother,' Yama said. 'What can this clown do to you? It is Nala and Damayanti you are testing. Nala has already submitted to his fate. The day Damayanti refuses Nala for his fate, you have won. This time I'm sure she will choose wisely. Nala is no longer the handsome king he was. He is a poor ugly dwarf. She would never choose that ugly dwarf over any of us.'

Hemanga knew the words of Yama were true. He could only pray Damayanti remain steadfast in her love.

24

Swayamvara Again

The next morning, Hemanga was perched at the top of the pillar in the Vidarbha's royal hall. He was apprehensive about how Damayanti would react when she saw Nala as Bahuka. Even a slight hesitation, a shadow of revulsion on her face would shatter Nala and would crack the foundation of the couple's love forever. That man did not deserve Damayanti, thought Hemanga. It was only her determination and love for Nala that was going to save them all. It wasn't Nala and Damayanti's love story. It was Damayanti's story of love. *What a woman*, Hemanga thought, feeling once again that he should have been born a human. Nala didn't know how lucky he was to be loved by Damayanti. The wise thing for her would be to marry any of the powerful kings or one of the three Gods. She could even escape the fate of humanity when Brahma wiped out the human race to start afresh if she married one of the immortals. The Gods were sure to tempt her again. An escape from the pain of a mundane earthly existence was nothing to scoff at. Tormented with conflicting emotions, Hemanga waited for Damayanti to arrive.

The kings had taken their respective seats. The three Gods were at their best and other suitors had lost hope seeing these three resplendent young men. Rituparna had plonked himself on a chair that appeared too puny for his huge body. He rested one hand on the curve of his bulging belly and ran the fingers of the other through his waist-length, salt-and-pepper beard. His bright eyes twinkled with amiable mischief and his face radiated confidence and goodwill. He would be happy if he got Damayanti, he would be happy if he didn't. He was just happy being himself. He sat enjoying the murmur of the crowd, breathing in the fragrance of the incense sticks, appreciating the intricate carvings of the pillar, and bursting with joy at every heartbeat.

In contrast, Nala stood puny and miserable like a rain drenched dog by his master's side. Hemanga could feel his anguish even from the distance. The shadow of Kali fell on the dwarf, making him appear more grotesque, if that was possible. The murmur in the hall died down suddenly and all eyes turn towards the inner door.

'My daughter Damayanti,' King Bhimasena announced. A collective sucking of air greeted the princess. Hemanga could see the wonder and lust in the eyes of the suitors. Nala moved behind Rituparna's chair, making himself as invisible as possible. Damayanti passed each king bowing and smiling at them before stepping forward. The scene was like the first swayamvara except for the presence of the three Gods in their own form.

Damayanti paused before Indra. The King of Gods bowed his head so that the princess could put the garland on his shoulders and welcome him to her life. She stepped forward to Agni and then to Yama and paused before Rituparna. The old man had not expected it. His eyes expanded in surprise as he stood up.

'Thank you,' Damayanti said, 'for everything you have done.'

'Devi, I don't know what I have done,' Rituparna said, confused, 'to deserve your thanks.'

Behind his chair, Nala stood frozen. A hiss of hot wind passed through the hall. Kali's shadow throbbed.

The three Gods watched intently as Damayanti stepped forward and touched Rituparna's feet. 'Bless us,' she said and pulled the dwarf out from his hiding place. Before anyone could react, she put the garland on Nala's shoulders and hugged him tightly. With a voice choking with emotion, she turned to her father and said, 'I have chosen my husband, Nala.' She turned triumphantly towards Rajguru and smiled at him.

'It is an insult. The kings have been humiliated,' Rajguru cried. That acted as a cue for the disgruntled kings who were seething with jealousy at their rejection by the beautiful princess. They rushed to finish off the dwarf. The swish of swords being drawn from the scabbards, the thump of the maces and abusive yells of the angry kings filled the air. Damayanti held Nala's arm tightly.

'If we die, we will die together,' Nala said.

'Die? Why should we die?' Damayanti asked and touched Rituparna's shoulders. 'Save us, noble king.'

Rituparna blinked, not comprehending what was happening but when a prince tried to thrust his dagger at Nala's throat, Rituparna struck him like lightning. Rituparna's slap sent the prince crashing to the wall. Another king swung his club like a maniac but Rituparna caught him by his waistband and flung him across the hall. The next few to attack, only remembered sitting dazed on the floor, holding their bleeding heads amidst the pillars that Rituparna had smashed their heads on. He was a one-man army. Rituparna lifted heavy seating implements and hurled them and threw many opponents against walls and pillars. The hall became a battlefield, with the massive Rituparna roaring like an angry bear at the centre.

The three Gods watched the fun and laughed uproariously. They encouraged Rituparna and applauded his punches, kicks, and slaps on the hapless scurrying kings who now wanted only to escape. The giant old man went through the rivals like a hungry elephant in a sugarcane field. Soon the wide front door of the royal hall was choked by the mob of panicked kings and princes fleeing from Rituparna's rage. They crowded at the gates, stumbling over each other, squeaking like mice desperate to exit their hole when chased by a cat. Rituparna pulled them one by one and beat them to a pulp.

The three Gods were there cheering the old king until the last of the suiters had managed to escape the hall, battered, purple-eyed and bruised. Rituparna stood at the door, his huge form filling the entire frame, and hurled choicest abuses at the fleeing kings.

'The lady has chosen her husband. Learn to respect the choice of the woman, you scoundrels, else I will teach you honour,' he thundered. 'The kings of Ayodhya have always done that.' Damayanti hugged him from behind and sobbed. He turned back and lifted her chin, 'Why are you crying now?'

'Thank you,' she whispered. Rituparna knelt before Nala, 'I am so happy for you, though I don't know why she has chosen you over me.'

'She is my wife,' Nala whispered.

'We were married long ago,' Damayanti added. She told him their story. Rituparna was moved to tears.

'I am sorry if I have treated you unfairly. I never knew you were a king,' he said to Nala.

'You were always kind,' Nala said, 'and I don't think you would have treated me any different even if you had known I was a king. I have never known you treating anyone any differently. You have always been kind to people.'

Rituparna roared in laughter. 'You are wrong, I treat everyone with equal disrespect and scorn.'

'On the contrary, you are . . .' but before Nala could complete, Rituparna cut him off with a gesture of his hand, 'You are not a poet or a bard that I have paid to spread lies about my character. So, spare me singing nonsense about myself. Now girl, who was the priest who had a problem with you marrying this man?'

Damayanti turned her head towards Rajguru and Rituparna walked towards him. The priest cowered. 'You have any problem?' Rituparna towered over the trembling priest.

'He . . . he is a Nishada,' Rajguru swallowed hard.

'So?'

'He is . . .' Rajguru gulped.

'Does it concern you, who the lady has chosen to live with?' Rituparna asked.

Gathering courage, the priest said, 'The shastras say . . .' he paused when he saw Rituparna crossing his hands across his broad chest, tapping his feet impatiently, and cocking an eyebrow to glare at the priest.

Rajguru squeaked, 'The shastras say when two people are in love, nothing else matters.' Rituparna glared at him.

'It really says so,' Rajguru said meekly, with open palms.

Slowly, a smile lit Rituparna's face. 'You are a learned man, Pandit.' Rituparna slapped Rajguru's shoulders jovially. 'Come to Ayodhya and we will have a discussion on the Vedas, Upanishads, and all. We will debate everything,' Rituparna winked, 'over Soma rasa and roasted wild boar.'

Before Rajguru could express his indignation at this offer, Rituparna hollered, 'Where are those three scoundrels? They were mocking me while I was fighting with all those stupid kings as if I were a prize bull in the ring needing encouragement. Where are they?'

The three Gods had vanished. Hemanga flew down from his perch and crying in joy said, 'They have gone, the Gods have gone!' Rajguru stared at him. 'A talking bird?'

Damayanti said, 'This was the messenger I mentioned. Our friend. Hemanga *hamsa*, the golden swan from heaven.'

Rituparna looked at the bird and then at Damayanti, 'Heaven? You have trained the bird well. He might be from some distant corner of the world. Heaven indeed!'

'I am from Brahma Loka, the heaven of Lord Brahma,' Hemanga said.

'Bah! Don't believe in the stories that bards tell. They are all liars. There is no other world than this earth.'

Hemanga was indignant but before he could start a heated argument, Damayanti said to Rituparna, 'We need your help, noble king.'

'Anything for you, Devi,' Rituparna bowed. 'Is there anyone who is still troubling you? I can deal with him now or is it some neighbouring king who is bothering you? I abhor war, but for you, I can send my army from Ayodhya.'

'It is not that easy,' Damayanti said. 'Kali, the God of misfortune, is angry with us.'

'There is no God of fortune or misfortune,' Rituparna asserted.

Damayanti looked thoughtful. She said, 'Perhaps you are right. Perhaps Kali is just the fear in our mind. But my husband is still afraid that misfortune stalks him.'

'Face it, man. Don't run from misfortune. Face it bravely.'

'He lost everything in gambling and . . .' Damayanti paused, looking at Nala.

Nala said, 'Whatever I lost in gambling I have to win back in the same way.'

'Says who?' Rituparna asked.

'That is the dharma.'

'Says who?' Rituparna scoffed.

Damayanti folded her hands in prayer and said, 'Teach my husband the game of dice.'

Rituparna scowled, 'The game of dice is not for the faint-hearted. If you play to win, you will lose. If you play to lose, then also you will lose. That is why it is said the game of dice is same as game of life.'

'Then how does one play this game?' Nala cried in despair.

'I will teach you, but before that, you must teach me something,' Rituparna's eyes twinkled with mischief. Nala waited for Rituparna to put forth his demand.

Rituparna said, 'Teach me Aswahridayamantra, the way to control the horses and make them run like wind.'

Nala grabbed Rituparna's hands and said, 'With pleasure, I will teach you.'

'Now.'

'Now,' repeated Nala with a joyous laugh.

Rituparna hurried out with an enthusiasm of a ten-year-old boy. Soon the Vidarbha palace grounds witnessed the strange scene of the dwarf teaching the giant the secret trick of making horses run as fast as the wind.

Hemanga sat beside Damayanti, watching the dare devilry of the old king. Then suddenly he noticed a dark shadow. It seemed to be galloping along with the horse Rituparna was riding. As he watched, the shadow stretched and Hemanga screamed in terror. A dark hand had grabbed Rituparna's legs. The next moment the old king was thrown from the saddle and he landed with a sickening thud. Nala ran to him, crying. Hemanga rushed to meet the inert figure of Rituparna lying sprawled on the ground.

'Is he dead? Is he dead?' the bird asked in a panic. The old man stirred a minute later and slowly sat up. He was covered in blood and there was a deep gash on his temple. Wiping the blood away from his beard, he once again mounted his horse and galloped. 'Beware of Kali, he is after you,' Hemanga cried. But the king didn't hear for he had shot forward on his horse. Kali's shadow followed the horse at great speed and this time tripped the horse but Rituparna jumped out of the saddle at the right moment and rolled away. The horse collapsed. Rituparna came back whispering something in the horse's ears, cajoling it with kindness. Soon he was galloping away at a great speed. He fell many times but got back to his feet every time with more vigour and enthusiasm.

Injury, the jeers of the crowd who had assembled to see the old man's clumsy attempts to ride the horse so fast, or even the desperate warnings of Hemanga to be careful about Kali— nothing stopped Rituparna. When the sun set, he was still riding. When it was midnight, he had changed horses but nothing could stop him from riding. He fell, got up, and rode again and again. By dawn, the jeering crowd had gone home tired. Nala was dozing, Hemanga had slept but Rituparna was still riding like a wind. Only Damayanti watched him but the old king did not care who watched. He rode and rode and rode again. By next noon he defeated Nala in a horse race and Damayanti cheered not for her husband but for the lovable eccentric. By the third day evening, there was no better rider than him and people were cheering for him. Rituparna didn't care for that either.

When the king came back with a triumphant smile, Damayanti congratulated and said, 'Now please teach my husband the art of gambling.'

In reply, Rituparna said, 'It is time to celebrate my achievement.' The whole night the king celebrated. Nala and

Damayanti waited impatiently for him to come back. The king slept for the next two days. On the third day, Rituparna woke up, had a hearty meal, washed it all down with copious soma rasa, and then sat before Nala to teach him the art of gambling.

'Play for the sake of playing. Neither the loss nor the win should affect you. Enjoy the game,' Rituparna said and stood up. 'The lesson is over.'

'That is it?' Hemanga cried.

'Now he needs to practise rolling the dice,' Rituparna said looking at Damayanti.

'Kali has rigged the dice with his black powers and his representative Dvapara is an ace player,' Nala cried.

'Look, son. There is no Kali or fate. If the dice is rigged, you should know it when you hold it in your hand. For that, you will need practice. So, practise, practise, practise, and when you are tired, practise again. Refuse to believe in mantras, charms, and all nonsense. Trust in yourself and make yourself worthy of your trust. Now sit and practise,' he roared.

Damayanti took the place Rituparna had vacated and took the dice, 'Now you will not stop until you have perfected your art,' she said to her husband.

It took three months for Nala to beat Rituparna the first time. Then it again took a year for him to beat Rituparna consistently. When Damayanti was confident that Nala could take on Dvapara, Rituparna rode them to the Nishada kingdom. Hemanga followed behind. He could see a bat flying ahead. Kali too was prepared for the final showdown.

25

Game with Kali

They entered the Nishada city on the festival day of Chithra Pournami. The city was decorated with festoons for the festival of the spring moon. Though the Nishadas appeared gloomy, the new masters of the city—the men Dvapara had brought—were in a festive mood. It was *their* festival.

The Nishada women, who were washing the streets and putting up decorations, stopped their work to stare at the chariot as it flew past them at a breakneck speed. Hemanga watched the city, sitting on the shoulders of Rituparna who had driven the chariot from Vidarbha with reckless abandon.

'The talking bird has come with a giant devil,' someone cried from a balcony. Then another saw Damayanti.

'The queen, the queen!' they cried. As the chariot careened through the streets, Nishada people defied their supervisor's command, threw away their brooms and baskets, and ran behind the chariot. The chariot stopped before the palace gate and Hemanga yelled at the guards, 'Open the gates! Your beloved king has arrived.'

'Nala, Nala!' It started as a whisper. 'Where is Nala?' They stared at the dwarf who was holding Damayanti's hand and looked at him suspiciously, 'This is not our Nala. Our king was so handsome,' said another.

'No, no, it is him only. Look at those eyes,' a woman argued.

'Silence! Go and work,' a soldier shouted at the Nishadas, but they ignored him.

Rituparna bellowed, 'Are you opening the gates, or shall I smash them open!?' The defiance of the giant old man brought cries of cheer and hooting from the crowd. No one had dared to talk to the Dvapara soldiers so boldly since the city had fallen.

'Break it down, break it down, and let King Nala in,' they chanted in unison.

Damayanti raised her hand to pacify the crowd. 'Patience my people,' she said. 'We have not come to fight. Nala has come to win against Kali.' That was a bold statement. Challenging the God of fate was not for the faint-hearted and the sheer audacity of it made the crowd go ecstatic. Hemanga could see the shadow shifting near the gate and slip inside the palace through the crack of the doors. A shudder passed through the spine of Hemanga. It was a matter of life and death for Kali. And he was not going to give up so easily.

The palace gate cracked open and Nala and Damayanti walked hand in hand, followed by a cheering crowd who assembled in the courtyard. The palace shook with the slogans hailing Nala. Soon Dvapara appeared at the balcony and the Nishadas booed. Beside him was Pushkara. He appeared dazed and stoned.

'There, look at that ugly dwarf. That is your brother Nala who has come to challenge you,' Dvapara said to Pushkara, pointing at Nala.

Pushkara could barely stand on his legs and held the balcony railing with trembling hands. 'Help me, brother,' he slurred. 'I have been tricked. I am under the thumb of this evil man.' Dvapara paled. He had certainly not expected this. The next moment Pushkara toppled from the balcony. Nala's brother landed on the courtyard with a sickening thud. Damayanti screamed.

Nala roared at Dvapara, 'You will pay for this! You evil monster, I challenge you to a game of dice.'

'I am coming,' Dvapara roared back, taking out the pair of dice from his waistband and clicking them together. Soon, they were sitting with the board of dyuta spread between them. The anxious Nishadas crowded around. Rituparna was the game supervisor. 'We will play with my pair of dice,' Dvapara said. He rolled the black pairs of dice and they vibrated with sinister energy.

'No, we will play with mine,' said Nala rolling the pair Rituparna had gifted him. The ivory dice of Ayodhya rolled with a pleasant clang. It was a stalemate before the game had even begun. Both refused to play with the other's pair. Nala knew if he used Dvapara's dice he was sure to lose, and Dvapara knew Nala knew the trick and both refused to budge.

'Then you go back the way you had come. Out. No game for you!' Dvapara smiled.

Damayanti said, 'Use one of Nala's dice and one of yours.'

Hemanga who was sitting beside the inert body of Pushkara was devastated at this suggestion 'What have you done, Devi,' he cried in dismay, 'Those dice of Dvapara has the soul of Kali. Even one is potent enough to destroy Nala. We are doomed.' Damayanti did not reply but sat with a worried face. There was no other choice for them if they wanted to play and hoped to win.

Dvapara agreed to Damayanti's suggestion. Nala took one of the black die of Dvapara in his hand and cried out in pain. The black die started glowing red and simmering in his palm. A whiff of black smoke escaped through the cracks between Nala's fingers. Soon the black die started glowing white-hot.

'What is at stake?' Dvapara asked, delaying the throw of dice as much as he could.

Nala, squirming in pain, said, 'The kingdom. The kingdom.'

'You have no kingdom, and I have no intention of staking what is mine. What else do you have?' Dvapara asked with deliberate slowness. Nala hesitated. He owned nothing. Kali's dice was burning through his skin.

'Stake me,' Damayanti cried 'I am yours, always. Stake me Nala.' Dvapara waited, running his fingers through his beard. His eyes glinted with malice. Hemanga knew what game Kali was playing.

'She is right,' Dvapara said, 'but I don't want her as my slave. I respect women. I am not like your brother who lusted after your wife. I am a Brahmachari.' Dvapara was stalling, making Nala suffer with the burning hot dice boring through his palm. As per the rules of the game, once a player had picked up the dice, he could only throw it after the stakes were agreed upon. If Nala threw it before that he would have lost the game.

'Tell what you want,' Rituparna growled.

'Well, let me think,' Dvapara said, scratching his chin. Nala gritted his teeth and tried hard not to throw the dice away. The smell of charred flesh spread in the air.

'I will count till three and if you have not put out your demand, I will declare Nala the winner.'

'Oh, that is not fair,' Dvapara said. 'If you have read what the dharma shastras have stated about dyuta . . .'

'One,' Rituparna began counting. The crowd hooted in happiness.

'Actually, there are rules, you cannot go against . . .' Dvapara cried. The crowd booed him.

'Two,' Rituparna shouted.

'Damayanti should marry me willingly. She should forsake Nala,' Dvapara said smiling at her. 'And if this ugly dwarf wins, he shall have everything back.' There was a dead silence. Hemanga knew he had lost. If Nala gave up, he lost the chance to play for another twelve years. But Nala would never stake Damayanti.

'It is alright, Nala,' Damayanti said with tearful eyes, 'Do it. I won't judge you. You lost everything, for my sake. Win that back.'

'Would that mean you have forsaken him?' Dvapara asked triumphantly.

'No,' Damayanti cried.

'Then how will you marry me willingly?' Dvapara asked.

Rituparna interfered. 'Enough. Nala has neither put her on stake, nor have you won so far. Is the condition acceptable to you, Nala?' Rituparna asked.

'No,' cried Nala.

'Then give up,' Dvapara spat.

'I have something else to stake,' Nala said.

'You don't even own the cloth you wear,' Dvapara sniggered.

'My life,' Nala said calmly, 'if I lose, you can hang me.'

Damayanti cried, 'No!'

'I stake my life,' Nala declared again.

Rituparna asked, 'Is it acceptable?'

The colour drained out of Dvapara's face. Hemanga did not know what changed the scenario but Dvapara nodded. Nala rolled the dice, and the game began.

As Nala's pieces advanced on the board, Hemanga knew that Dvapara had been outsmarted. Slowly it dawned on him. He remembered Nala's lament that he could not even die because of the curse of Kali.

Nala had staked his life. He was invincible till Kali's curse remained. Kali had no choice other than to remove the curse if he wanted to defeat Nala. Kali left with no choice, was doing just that because if Dvapara won, he would have to kill Nala, but if the curse of Kali was there, Nala was immortal. The crowd watched with wonderstruck eyes as the ugly dwarf was changing form before their eyes. With every successive roll of the dice, Nala's limbs grew, his misshapen face straightened to the original handsome shape, and when the final fort of Dvapara in the dyuta board fell, the crowd saw the handsome Nala manifest in his full glory before their eyes. The crowd cheered with happiness.

Dvapara fell back dead, and a thick black smoke curled up from his ears and nostrils. As they watched, the body of Dvapara disintegrated into countless black specs. They collated to form a giant bat, and an ear-splitting screech filled the air. It exploded, sending shock waves across the surrounding space.

The shadow of Kali disappeared from the Nishada kingdom forever.

The crowd cried in unison, 'Jai Nala Maharaj, Jai Rani Damayanti.' Hemanga circled the city, somersaulting in the air, croaking with joy, and for the first time, no one complained about his harsh voice or his singing. They were busy celebrating the return of their just king. Damayanti was in Nala's embrace while a beaming Rituparna stood beside them. Hemanga saw Pushkara waking up as if from sleep. Kali had promised to give back everything to Nala if he had won. Everything, including the brother. Hemanga flew back and landed near the couple.

Damayanti hugged the bird and said, 'Thank you for being such a friend.' Amavasi, who had hidden in the chariot all along, found his place back at Damayanti's feet. Hemanga patted the excellent dog and got a wet squeaky lick in return. He squirmed, but today he would suffer even Amavasi's licking. Today was the day it was proved that humans, too, were capable of selfless love. He couldn't wait to see Brahma's face when he narrated the triumph of true love to him.

Rituparna was saying goodbye, 'Well played, son. Now remember the mantra of life: eat, drink, and enjoy.' The Nishadas roared in unison, 'Life is short but sweet, enjoy every moment.'

The good old king left the couple to their bliss. His chariot sped back to Ayodhya, spilling with gifts and many young Nishadas. They were singing with Rituparna, 'No God, no demon, no tomorrow, no yesterday. There is now and now is true. Eat, drink, and enjoy. Heaven is here and now!'

Hemanga knew his time to part had come. He kissed goodbye to the couple and circled the city once more before soaring to Brahma Loka. On the way, in a dark valley, he saw Kali lurking in the shadows howling like a wounded wolf. Hemanga couldn't resist meeting the God of fate one last time. He was no longer scared of Kali.

'Curse be upon you, bird,' Kali screamed when he saw him, 'Don't think you have won. I shall stalk humans, hound their dreams, dwell in their fears, and whisper evil thoughts in their ears. I will bring wars, pestilence, and epidemics. I will light the fire of envy and greed in their mind, and humanity will suffer with me forever.'

'Hah, you fool,' Hemanga said, 'God of fate, your fate is to lose. For the weak may pray, the fools may fight, but as long as there are men like Rituparna who believe in themselves and refuse to believe in you, and as long as women like Damayanti are there who refuse to give up, and men like Nala who can stake their lives for their loved ones, you will never succeed. You have no power over humanity. Send war and messengers of peace will arise. Send epidemics, and they will find a cure.

Weigh them down with despair and they will soar with hope. Send them giant ocean waves, and they will learn to surf over them. And you will always remain the clown.'

Kali gave a howl of pain and rage—it hurt to hear the truth. The golden bird rose high over the earth that was bathed in the glory of the rising sun. The bird felt a final pang of pity for the God of fate as it soared above and across the glorious light of the victory and warmth; the wail of Kali ebbing away softly into oblivion.

Epilogue

Hemanga reached his flock with fantastic tales of his adventure. Nobody believed him. 'No human could defeat Gods, let alone the powerful God of fate,' they said. He became the laughingstock among his friends. The poor bird sulked. He went to Brahma and sobbed before the creator, 'They don't believe me after all I have done.'

Brahma patted the golden swan's head and said, 'Poor bird, you cry because they don't believe you. Look at me.'

Hemanga looked at the creator with perplexed eyes, 'Who was the one who inspired you in your little adventure?' asked Brahma. *Little adventure indeed*, Hemanga fumed, but he didn't dare to voice out the resentment to Brahma. He pondered over Brahma's question. He loved Damayanti, Nala, and even Amavasi, but the one who inspired him was...

'Rituparna, the insane!' cried Hemanga.

'Ha! One of my best creations,' Brahma said.

'But he doesn't believe in you or heaven. He calls them all nonsense.'

'Nonsense?'

'I mean,' Hemanga gulped.

Brahma roared in laughter, 'All the more reason for me to love him. It isn't important that humans believe in me or such nonsense. It is only important that they believe in themselves.'

Hemanga blinked, not understanding half of what the creator was saying. He asked slowly, 'And if they don't believe in themselves?'

'Well, then they would have invited Kali to their lives,' Brahma said, laughing aloud. Hemanga had to smile at that. It was true. He wished no one would ever have Kali in their life.

'Now, my little son,' Brahma said, patting the golden bird, 'Don't worry about your friends not believing in you. As long as I am alive . . .'

'What? Do you also die?'

'You won't allow me to finish, will you? I will also die one day, and a new Brahma will come. The only immortal thing is change. But, as long as I am alive and the world exists, the tale of Nala and Damayanti will be told.'

It filled Hemanga's heart, and tears spurted from his eyes for no apparent reason.

Brahma said in a kind voice, 'And when poets recount their eternal tale again and again, who would be the hero of the story?'

'Nala?' Hemanga asked, his heartbeat thudding in his ribcage.

'Well. Maybe for some poets, Nala could be the hero. For some, it would be Damayanti, and some may even prefer Rituparna. But for me, the eternal messenger of love is the hero of this tale.' Brahma winked at the golden swan.

Hemanga rushed to the embrace of Brahma and buried his face in the chest of his father. Between his tears, he asked, 'Can I sing?'

And Brahma sighed and said, 'Alright.'